MURDER ON THORNTON MOUNTAIN

J T ONEY

Sale of this book without the cover may be unauthorized. If this book is coverless it may have been reported to the publisher as "unsold or destroyed" and neither the author nor the publisher may have received payment for it.

This book is a work of fiction. Names, characters, businesses, organizations, places, events, and incidents either are the product of the author's imagination or are used fictitiously. Any resemblance to actual persons, living or dead, events, or locations is entirely coincidental. All characters in this book are fictitious and any resemblance to persons living or dead is purely coincidental.

Copyright © 2012 by J T Oney

All rights reserved. Printed in the United States of America. No part of this book may be reproduced in any manner whatsoever without the written permission of the author except for brief quotations embodied in critical articles or reviews.

CreateSpace ISBN

ISBN-13: 9781480036383
ISBN-10: 1480036382

For my brother, LTC Bill Oney.
He showed us the way.

Also by J.T. Oney

Mutterings of a Madman:
Letters to My Family on War and Politics

Betrayal at Saint-Etienne

Morgan's Mountain

Also by J. T. Oney: *Betrayal at Saint Etienne*

Capt. Thomas Hunt Morgan makes his appearance in *Murder on Thornton Mountain* and is descended from a long line of mountain men who picked up a rifle to defend their country.

This is the story of his grandfather, Maj. John Hunt Morgan, who fought in World War II. When the Japanese bombed Pearl Harbor, Morgan knew he would have to leave his family to become an infantryman, just as his father had done during World War I.

He possessed the language and fighting skills the army needed: the skills to parachute into occupied France and organize French resistance in preparation for the Normandy invasion. The Office of Strategic Services (OSS) needed such men and recruited him for behind-the-line operations.

He reported to the Q building in D.C., where he was assigned to Area F for his initial training, then to Area B for more advanced training. At Area B he first makes the acquaintance of Maj. W. E. Fairborn, a British Special Operations Executive (SOE) officer responsible for turning OSS agents into lethal killing machines.

When shipped to England to complete his training, Morgan was selected for the Jedburghs, who were organized into three-man teams to be dropped into France to organize the French maquis to keep the Nazi from sending reinforcements to repel the invasion of Normandy.

When his team, Team Abigail, was dropped by parachute into occupied France, he knew it was time to kill or be killed.

Also by J. T. Oney: *Morgan's Mountain*

In 1780, Maj. John Booth Morgan rode into the Watauga settlement, where he was to serve with Col. John Sevier in the frontier militia guarding against Indian attacks. While he was there, Alifair Leandro asked him to escort her though the Cumberland Gap into the wilds of *Kain-tuc-kee.*

However, before their trip, the Revolutionary War came to the south, and Morgan rode with his cousins and the Over the Mountain Men to fight Patrick Ferguson at the Battle of Kings Mountain.

Not long after he returned to the Watauga settlement, Morgan's uncle, Daniel Morgan, sent for him and the Long Rifles of the Frontier Militia to support him at the Battle of the Cowpens.

During the battle, Morgan was wounded while saving General Green from capture and spent several months recuperating before finally leaving for Kentucky.

Indian trouble, however, was on the horizon. Morgan, accompanied by his cousins Willis and Lacie would need all their fighting skills just to survive.

CHAPTER 1

HOMECOMING

Capt. Thomas Hunt Morgan, recently of Afghanistan, boarded the bus in Hazard, Kentucky, and sat relaxed in the right front seat so he could talk to the driver, a man named Big Stride Walker. He was on his way home. He felt like hell, and he did not look much better. He was a thin six-footer with close-cut hair. He sported a livid scar that ran from just above his right eye, cutting a half-moon to end at the right side of his chin.

He had just been discharged from the veterans' hospital in Lexington, Kentucky, and was thirty pounds below his normal weight. He was limping slightly; his left leg was like a gravel pit because of shrapnel holes caused by a grenade.

The hospital provided good services to the wounded, but it was no place to gain weight. The food was passable, but not for Morgan, who was looking forward to a meal of beans, potatoes, and cornbread. He was dressed in army desert boots, jeans, a long-sleeve cotton shirt, and a waist-length, dark-blue barn coat similar to the one his grandfather used to wear. His head was covered by a muddy-colored bill cap proclaiming, "I Support Coal."

During her last visit, his wife, Rachel, had brought the clothes for him to wear home. She had volunteered to drive to Lexington and pick him up, but he was looking forward to the bus ride—the same ride his father and grandfather had taken home.

He had once known Big Stride's first name, but could not recall it.

Big Stride had looked at Morgan as he boarded the bus. "Morgan, you look like something the cat dragged in."

For as long as he could remember everyone had called him Morgan. His first name was Thomas Hunt, but everyone seemed comfortable calling him by his last name. He merely grunted his assent. "Big Stride, I don't feel much better than I look."

"War is a bitch, Morgan, but you boys seem to like it. You know, I always seem to be bringing you boys home. I remember bringing your daddy home from Vietnam. My daddy said he remembered bringing your grandfather home during World War II and your uncle from the Korean War.

"When your daddy came home, the country was in real turmoil, and there was really no one except your mother, a few Coeburn kin, and the sheriff there to greet him. Looks like it's going to be the same for you—just the Leandro woman, her mother, and the sheriff will be there."

"Big Stride, that sounds plenty. I never did like crowds."

"I assume with the sheriff being there it means you'll take your old job back." Morgan had been a deputy sheriff for Logan County when he left two years before.

"Yeah, Big, I like the job, and I like working for the sheriff. Except for my time in the military, that is about all I've ever done. Hell, the truth is that's about all I've ever been good at."

"Morgan, it doesn't seem right. A soldier with your kind of medals ought to have a marching band waiting. What did you do with those medals anyway?"

Morgan paused. "Rachel put them in a drawer somewhere."

"Morgan, I asked your daddy the same about his and, as I recall, got the same response."

Morgan turned and looked out the window at the redbuds just starting to bloom on the hillside. "Big, it's nice to be recognized for doing a good job. But it's never about honor, country, or patriotism. Those things are overrated in combat. What's important are the boys next to you. They are the people you trust and are as close to you as your family. And you fight for them just as hard as you fight for your family."

As the bus came to the top of the mountain and started down the hill, Morgan caught a glimpse of the small town through the barren trees, which were just starting to bud after the harsh mountain winter. There was not much room between the hills for a town to grow, so it had spread along the Kentucky River. It was not a big town, but it was large by mountain standards, since it served as the seat of Logan County. He smiled and thought, *At least it's big enough for two stoplights and a courthouse.*

In front of the courthouse stood a statue of a Civil War soldier. Morgan never could figure out whether it was blue or gray, and he didn't figure it mattered. The town was honoring a soldier, and that was good enough.

As the bus pulled up to the courthouse, three people were waiting: Rachel, the sheriff, and the county judge, who was also Rachel's mother. Morgan limped off the bus and into Rachel's arms. He hugged her as she kissed him on his cheek. He expected that and didn't mind because he knew the Leandro women were not much for showing emotion in public.

He took her by the shoulders and looked at her. He was always amazed at how he felt toward this woman. Rachel was typical of the Leandro woman—small, thin, and bony with hair as black as a Campbell's heart and skin the color of leaves on an aspen tree in spring. They all had violet eyes—eyes that could drown you with love or strike fear with a flash.

The Leandro women had also always been the smartest and best-educated women he had ever encountered. As far back as he could remember, they had controlled the county, sometimes in the light, sometimes from the shadows. Somewhere in the distant past the Leandro women had gained the trust and respect of the people and had never lost it.

The judge came up and he put his left arm around her and hugged them both as she kissed him on the left check. He looked at both the mother and daughter and knew then why the Leandro women were so prized.

The sheriff looked him over as he shook his hand. "You look poorly, Morgan. After Rachel gets some meat on your bones, come by and visit with me."

Morgan promised he would and turned back to Rachel as the sheriff and the judge walked back to the courthouse. They both knew it was time to leave them alone.

As they walked toward her Jeep, she told him they were going to the new house and not to the trailer. When Morgan had left, they were sharing a trailer. He smiled and thought, *That's all I could afford.* During his absence, she had wanted to build a new house for them on a small plateau near the top of the mountain. The new house was about ten miles from town and about five miles from the Piney Branch Medical Clinic, which she managed and where she practiced medicine.

Morgan was a dumb mountain man but not dumb enough to say no, so the house had been built. He did not feel bad about her paying for it, because he knew she and her mother were principals in the Leandro Foundation, which was a massive, nonprofit, international education and health enterprise. He had not yet seen the cabin but was looking forward to it, since she was excited about it.

They drove out of town and turned to go up the mountain to the new cabin. Several white trucks were parked along the road. When Morgan looked at them questioningly, Rachel said, "Something new and controversial since you have been gone. The drilling trucks belong to the Humboldt Company. They intend to open a new gas well on Thornton Mountain."

They drove quickly up the mountain until they reached a switchback that had a turnoff onto a narrow blacktop road.

Morgan liked the view from the road, for as they drove he could see for miles across the valleys and mountains. The view was unbroken except for several mountains barren of trees and vegetation due to hilltop mining. He always wanted summer to come early to cover the mountain scars. He was also a little embarrassed at the unsightly mountain scars, but he knew they were a necessary product of his people's attempt to make a living.

They went around a curve, and Rachel stopped the Jeep so he could see the cabin. A hundred yards in front of them stood a two-story, log house nestled in a grove of silver maples. The cabin was made of brown logs chinked with white daubing. The low western sun framed the cabin and trees. The back of the cabin faced west and had a porch that overlooked the mountains. On the other side of the cabin, at the end of the drive, was a two-story garage, separate from the cabin. In front of the garage was Morgan's old truck.

He nodded to Rachel and simply said, "It's a beautiful place. It reminds me of Grandma's cabin."

She squeezed his hand and said, "I'm glad you're pleased. I like it as well. It reminds me of my grandparents' cabin also. I was happy there, but I'm happier here."

As they walked into the cabin, he asked her to show him around. She stopped, took off his coat, and said, "Later." She put her arms around his neck and welcomed him home.

CHAPTER 2

THE SUDAN

Morgan had been home for a month, and some of the night restlessness he had initially experienced was slowly leaving him. He no longer rose and walked about the house or sat on the porch, drank chai, and stared unseeing at the moon.

He was starting to walk the old Indian paths that ran across the mountain in back of the new cabin. The paths were a little overgrown but still passable. Soon the leaves would cover the trees and once more hide the paths. One of the Coeburn boys or Ancil would sometimes suddenly appear out of the woods and walk with him.

The Coeburn boys, Denver, Virgil, and Mason, were his cousins, and he had grown up with them. He liked all his cousins—especially Virgil and Ancil, who had served with him on three military deployments. While Morgan was recovering at the veterans' hospital, Virgil had resumed his job as a deputy sheriff while Ancil resumed roaming the mountains.

It was obvious that Rachel had called them and given them their orders. They did not resent her orders, for they had been receiving them since childhood. They always laughed about it but then did what she asked.

When Virgil walked with him through the woods, they always stopped every mile or so and practiced with their pistols or knives. While serving together in Sudan, Iraq, and Afghanistan, they had developed a number of exercises to maintain or increase their skills. From experience, each knew that constant exercise was the key to being skilled. The ability to get into action without thought had saved both their lives on numerous occasions.

At one of their shooting sessions, they began to relive one of the incidents that had demonstrated to them the necessity of honing their skills. Prior to deployment to Afghanistan, they had been posted to Darfur to assess the capabilities of the Janjaweed, who were raiding and killing the local non-Muslims. Morgan had just been promoted to captain, and Virgil was his senior sergeant, while Ancil was his scout.

Morgan had six other Shooters with him. They were all dressed in desert uniform and wore tan berets. Their uniforms had no rank insignia, and each man was heavily armed. They stopped at a walled farmyard, where several correspondents and a contingent of soldiers from the Netherlands were staying. Virgil motioned for the Shooters to position themselves around the farm while he and Morgan talked with the reporters and the lieutenant from the Netherlands. Ancil, as usual, was in a hide, nowhere in sight.

After gathering what information they could, Morgan and Virgil sat under a small overhang on a straw mat, talking to the newsmen and drinking coffee. A truck stopped outside the gate to the farm, and fifteen men dressed in Sudanese uniforms came through the gate. The major in charge was tall and slender with a small mustache. He carried a swagger stick in the British fashion, which he continually tapped against his leg. In a loud, commanding voice he began to speak to the Netherlands lieutenant, demanding that the local farmers be turned over to him.

Morgan and Virgil continued to drink their coffee and listen to the major harangue the lieutenant. The major claimed the farmers were terrorists and had been supporting the rebels in the area. Morgan could see the Netherlands officer was wavering and intended to turn the local farmers over to the major and his soldiers. He knew if that happened, they would be slaughtered like farm animals.

Morgan looked at Virgil. "Never happen," he said and rose to his feet. Virgil rose and raised his left hand in a clenched fist. The Shooters positioned themselves around the farm, unnoticed by either the Sudanese or Netherlands soldiers, and maneuvered into firing position.

Morgan walked to where the major and the lieutenant were talking and wanted to know what the lieutenant was going to do. The lieutenant indicated he had no authority to prevent the major from taking the farmers.

Morgan looked at him and said, "Sure you do." He turned to the major and told him the farmers were under his protection and to leave the farmyard. The major struck Morgan in the face with his swagger stick and told Morgan he wanted the farmers turned over to him.

Morgan, blood dripping down his face, smiled at him and said, "Not today."

He then drew his pistol and shot the major between the eyes. The Netherland soldiers went to the ground while the Sudanese soldiers started to bring their weapons into action. Morgan began to fire his pistol as fast as he could aim into the packed Sudanese soldiers. Just as Morgan killed the major, Virgil began to fire his shotgun while the Shooters, positioned around the farmyard, poured automatic fire into the Sudanese soldiers.

In less than ten seconds, the firing began to die down with only sporadic fire from the Shooters as they finished off the Sudanese soldiers that had continued to fight. In a low voice, Morgan said to Virgil, "Cease fire."

Virgil raised his left hand, palm outward, and waved it back and forth. The firing ceased immediately. Morgan pointed at three of the Shooters and then toward the downed Sudanese soldiers. The three ran into the open area and began to check the Sudanese soldiers to make sure they were either dead or completely out of action. The remaining Shooters stayed in their shooting positions to provide cover for those doing the checking.

Morgan quickly checked on the Shooters to make sure no one was down. He then checked the newsmen and the soldiers from the Netherlands. Everyone seemed to be unhurt.

In the meantime, Ancil had come down from his hide and was also checking on the downed soldiers by prodding them with a knife. He raised his head, waved his hand, and, with his knife, pointed to a soldier who was still alive. Morgan shook his head for Ancil not to kill him and pointed with his left hand toward the farmhouse. Ancil put his knife back into his scabbard and, assisted by one of the Shooters, put plastic cuffs on the prisoner, raised him to his feet, and dragged him toward the farmhouse.

The Netherlands lieutenant had recovered by this time and began to shout at Morgan about murdering the Sudanese soldiers. Morgan turned to him and told him to shut up. The lieutenant continued to scream threats. Morgan drew his pistol, pointed it at the lieutenant's head, and told him once more to shut up. The Shooters again moved into shooting position. The lieutenant immediately went silent.

As they recalled the aftermath of the fight, Virgil and Morgan looked at each other and laughed. Unbeknownst to Morgan, a newsman had filmed the entire incident, and for the next few weeks it was shown on the nightly news, with the liberal stations proclaiming murder and the conservative stations proclaiming justice. The incident became known as the Fight at the Farm.

The lieutenant had formally written up a charge against Morgan, which was quickly dropped and forgotten. Immediately after the firefight, Ancil had interrogated the captured soldier, who indicated the major was supporting the Janjaweed.

The colonel commanding Morgan's unit was a grizzled veteran of thirty years and two wars who, after watching the video, had called Morgan and Virgil into his office and poured three glasses of moonshine, conveniently provided by Virgil. He gave one to Morgan and the other to Virgil and raised his glass with the comment "Morgan, Virgil, I wish to hell I had been there." Both knew he meant it.

Morgan and Virgil had always agreed that he was the best commanding officer they had ever served under. He led from the front and allowed nothing to roll down onto the troops he commanded.

CHAPTER 3

CHIEF DEPUTY SHERIFF

The next morning, Rachel looked at Morgan and indicated it was time for him to see the sheriff and go back to work. He recognized the expression on her face; she was tired of him hanging around the house and taking up her time. He was glad for her nudge, because he had started to feel his energy rising and knew it was time to see the sheriff.

That afternoon Morgan climbed into his truck and started the short drive down the mountain. The afternoon sun was casting shadows on the road, and occasionally Morgan glanced out the left window at the hazy, blue mountains in the distance. Over the mountainside, now showing some of its summer color, he could spot small groupings of houses low in the hollers, squatting patient and tired next to a dirt road. The streams beside each dirt road gradually found their way to the Kentucky River.

When he was away, he always missed the hills, the people, and the mountain culture. It was different from the rest of the country, he admitted, but he mused that each part of the country had been settled by a different stream of immigrants from different countries.

Morgan laughed. *Hell,* he thought, *every section of the country is a nation in itself.* He knew his ancestors came from the Scottish Highlands, had traveled down the Old Wagon Trail that was now Route 81 in Virginia and settled in the Yadkin Valley of North Carolina, before coming though the Cumberland Gap and spreading across the mountains.

It was a family legend that one of his ancestors had brought a Leandro woman with him when he had crossed the mountains. It was possible, he thought, because the Morgan men were always partial to good-looking, intelligent women. The Morgan men always seemed to perk up when that kind of woman came around. He smiled as he thought of Rachel.

He liked his family and knew they liked him. It was a large extended family; he figured he was related to half the people in the county. Most importantly, they were loyal to one another. They might occasionally fight among themselves, but it was rarely over a killing matter.

Generally they fought one another because they just felt good—and they seemed to feel good a lot. That was especially true of him and his cousins. They liked and respected one another, but sometimes they just felt good. When trouble came, he knew the family would stand together. It had been that way even before they had come through the gap in the mountains, and it was that way now. *Damn,* he thought, *it feels good to belong to such a family.*

As Morgan drove down the mountain, he was constantly alert to the traffic around him, especially the heavy, overloaded coal trucks that crawled up and down the winding mountain road that crossed from Logan County into Beech County. In the winter months, the mountain trees were always covered with snow, and the roads could be treacherous for all vehicles, especially during heavy fog that rose from the valley floor and clung to the mountaintops.

Several hundred yards along the left side of the road, he saw Whit Vance standing alongside his mailbox. His real name was Whitcomb Vance, but most his neighbors called him Whit or Ims.

Morgan remembered his father at the dinner table, telling the story of how Whit got his nickname. As his dad began the story, his mother began to quarrel with him for telling it. Morgan and the other children always enjoyed this teasing, because they knew how much their father enjoyed hearing their mother's voice. It wasn't until Morgan met and married Rachel that he realized how common that was between people who enjoyed each other's company.

His father related that Whit had been out hunting for rabbits to put meat on the table when he ran across a moonshine still. He soon forgot about hunting and spent most of the day at the still. Finally, Homer Combs, who owned the still, came back and threatened to shoot Whit unless he went home.

When Whit got home, his wife had locked the door and wouldn't let him in, because she knew he'd be drunk. She wanted to know if he had brought any rabbit meat. He stood at the door, weaving back and forth, and said, "Ims got rabbits behind my back. Guess how many Ims got and Ims will give you both." The table always erupted in laughter after such tales by their father.

Morgan pulled up next to Whit and inquired, "How you doing, Whit?"

"Good, Morgan, fit as a fiddle, little out of tune but fine. Heard you were back from the war. Going back to sheriffing?"

Morgan nodded. He knew what the response was going to be, but he asked anyway: "Whit, why are you standing out here?"

"Why, waiting for the mail lady."

Morgan asked why, and Whit replied, "I'm waiting for my check."

Morgan asked innocently, "What check?"

Looking incredulously at Morgan, Whit replied, "Why, the one the mail lady brings every month."

Morgan replied that she was about a mile behind him. He waved at Whit and drove on down the hill. Morgan smiled to himself. He would enjoy relaying his conversation with Whit to Rachel over the dinner table that night, even though she'd heard it before.

It was about one o'clock when Morgan walked into the sheriff's office and greeted Mable Handshoe, the sheriff's office manager. Her thick glasses made her look owlish, and her flying hair made her look disorderly, but Morgan admired and liked her. He knew her to be one of the most intelligent and organized women he had ever met. She could find anything on the computer or by picking up the telephone and asking one of her friends. Morgan knew she was part of a vast network of law enforcement and intelligence personnel that shared information on an unofficial basis.

Mable began to fuss over him as she always did. He hugged her and kissed her cheek and asked if the sheriff was in.

She replied, "He's been waiting for you."

Sheriff Harley was sitting behind his desk with a telephone to his ear. He motioned for Morgan to take a seat. The room was stark, even by mountain standards. There were no photographs or "I love me" trophies on the walls or shelves, although Morgan knew that the sheriff could have filled all three walls with his awards. For him, the job was enough, and everyone respected him for that.

Harley finished his call, stood up, walked around the desk, and seated himself in an overstuffed chair next to Morgan. After he was seated, Mable walked into the room, carrying two cups of coffee and put one on the small table in front of the sheriff. She looked at Morgan before putting the cup in front of him, "Black, no sugar or cream, right?" Morgan nodded his thanks, and she left the room.

Morgan took a sip, smiled, and looked at the sheriff, who simply shrugged as if to say, "I don't know how she does it either." Being mountain men, they just accepted their good fortune and went on with their business.

The sheriff had occupied the same office as far back as Morgan could recall. When Rachel had returned to the mountains after medical school, Morgan had received his discharge from the military and had followed her back home. Sheriff Harley had offered him the same deputy sheriff's badge his father had worn. Except for his time away to serve with the military on various deployments in Africa, Iraq, and Afghanistan, he rose steadily in rank through the department. They trusted, respected, and were loyal to one another.

Without preliminaries, Harley placed Morgan's old badge on the coffee table and told him wanted him to be his chief deputy.

Morgan was glad to have the new position and responsibilities and expressed his appreciation. They continued the discussion, with Morgan highlighting several changes he would want to implement over the next couple of years. Morgan indicated he wanted Virgil to be his lead sergeant and to bring Ancil aboard as a civilian with full police powers. He wanted to build a training facility, to begin a regular training schedule, and to base future hires primarily on military combat service. The sheriff nodded and was pleased that Morgan had suggested the changes, for long ago he had decided that Morgan would be his replacement.

When Morgan left the sheriff's office, Mable presented him with several forms to sign. She had already filled out the required information, so Morgan did not even glance at the forms before signing them.

He was now officially the new chief deputy sheriff of Logan County and was looking forward to protecting his people from each other and from outsiders. Like most mountain men, he was old-fashioned and put great value on the family, God, and honor. His father and uncle had trained him well, he thought, for like Sheriff Harley, he knew that the law must be enforced with common sense and justice.

CHAPTER 4

GUNFIGHT AT THE MOUNTAIN GRILL

It was 0600 in the morning on Wednesday, and Morgan lay propped in bed, looking at his e-mails on his iPad. He had three e-mail accounts: one was for the sheriff's office, which he used only for official business; one for selected friends and relatives, on Gmail; and a third that was encrypted, and no one but he and Rachel knew about it. Morgan did not fully trust e-mail, so he and Rachel encrypted their personal communication to prevent others from spying on their relationship.

Rachel had been up for about an hour and was getting an early start to the clinic. She came into the bedroom and sat on the side of the bed. She did not say a thing but simply ran her hands up his chest to his face, placed both hands on each side of his face, and began to kiss him. He moaned low in his throat as she bit into the side of his neck.

As she pulled back, he muttered softly to her, "You sure know how to stir a man's blood."

As she began to get up, she placed her hand on the right side of his body and slowly scraped her nails along his stomach. His body involuntarily jerked a couple of times.

She looked at him, winked, and said, "See you tonight."

He soon heard her car start and slowly move out of the driveway.

It was impossible to continue answering e-mail, and he was not going to make his own breakfast, so he reached for his phone and called Virgil.

Angel, who was Virgil's current girlfriend, answered. She laughed softly when Morgan asked for Virgil. "Morgan, Virgil is tired and needs his rest."

"Angel, tell the Rooster to meet me at the Mountain Grill for breakfast, and tell him that it's on me."

Angel laughed again and said she would.

Morgan was seated in the back booth of the grill, talking to Jessica, when Virgil entered. Jessica was one of Morgan's cousins and a confidential informant.

Since becoming chief deputy, he had visited almost every establishment in the county and had gradually built up an intelligence network of confidential informants throughout the county. Most were waitresses, barbershop owners, and garage mechanics that he did small favors for in exchange for information on what the people in the county were doing or thinking. He knew from experience that this type of information could prevent angry words from resulting in violence. He knew the mountain people could be short-tempered and have long memories when they felt wronged.

Virgil came over, sat down, and immediately began to flirt with Jessica, even though she was kin, had two kids, and was happily married. Virgil called it harmless mountain flirting, which made both parties feel better about themselves. Jessica was giving him as good as she got while at the same time taking their orders.

Morgan smiled at the banter and envied Virgil for something he could never master, something he felt was a failing. He also knew that people were a little afraid of him, but that was simply his personality. There was nothing he could do or intended to do about it.

As they sat waiting for breakfast, Virgil entertained Morgan with his latest adventures. He was a good storyteller and seemed to take great pleasure in embellishing his tales. Morgan liked Virgil and the stories, so he sat quietly, observed the room, and listened with one ear as Virgil's tales got wilder and wilder.

Morgan noted that the county supervisor, Roy Thacker, sat at his usual table by the fireplace, engrossed in the *Mountain Herald* newspaper while he ate breakfast. Several tables away sat Old Man Wilson and three of his boys, talking animatedly among themselves while looking at Thacker.

Morgan muttered, "Crap." He knew Thacker had recently had a run-in with Old Man Wilson on a tax problem, because Wilson felt the government had no business taking his money, since it was needed to feed his family. He sympathized with the old man, but he knew he could be unreasonable. Trouble was coming, and his sons would go along with whatever the old man wanted to do.

Jessica came to the table and put the ticket on it with her left hand while squeezing Morgan's shoulder with her right. He read the note she had placed underneath the ticket and then put it in his coat pocket. Virgil looked at him questioningly.

"Jessica overheard Old Man Wilson talking about meeting the county supervisor out front."

Virgil nodded and resumed his eating.

When the county supervisor started to get up, Morgan reached into his wallet, pulled out two fifty-dollar bills, and dropped them on the table. He felt good as he did so. His wallet always seemed to contain extra money. Every time it became empty, money automatically appeared in his wallet by the next morning. *Having a rich wife does have advantages,* he thought as he smiled to himself.

They were five yards behind the county supervisor when they left the building. Morgan handed his truck keys to Virgil and told him to get the Remington 12-gauge pump shotgun behind the front seat. As he turned, Morgan told him it was loaded with alternating slugs and 00 buckshot with extra shells in the glove box. Virgil grunted acknowledgement and walked toward the truck as Morgan followed the county supervisor into the parking lot. He touched the .45 high on his right hip and felt comforted.

Old Man Wilson and his sons came from behind their truck and walked toward the county supervisor, who seemed surprised and took several steps back when the old man pointed his finger at him and began to curse him angrily for taking money that he needed to feed his family.

Morgan stopped just in front of and to the right of the supervisor and told the old man, "Stop this foolishness and go see the judge if you have a complaint with Thacker." The old man lowered his hand and voice. He knew Morgan was fair but was also known to be mean in a fight.

Morgan noticed the tenseness of Jason, the oldest son, just to the right of his father, and he knew immediately that he could be a problem. Morgan had known him since their teenage years, when they had hunted the hills together. Jason was a freak, whose muscles were twitchy fast and, in their youth, could draw and fire faster than anyone, including Morgan. Despite their youthful friendship, Jason had developed a wild streak over the last several years.

Morgan looked at Jason and shouted, "Don't do it, Jason!" Jason's shoulder rose as his eyes changed.

Morgan's hand immediately swept back and dropped to his pistol. He jumped the pistol up, bent his elbow so his weapon pointed toward Jason, and fired his first round. Before he could fire his second, he was forced back by the impact of Jason's bullet on his vest. He pushed his weapon forward and fired his second round as his left hand sought a two-hand grip. He then fully extended both arms into an isosceles stance and fired his third and fourth shots. Jason went slack and dropped to the pavement.

Morgan's focus had been on Jason, but now he turned his attention to Old Man Wilson and his other two sons. They had drawn their weapons and were firing at both him and Thacker. He heard Thacker cry out in pain and go to the pavement.

In the meantime, Virgil's shotgun began to boom from his right, and both sons jerked as if hit by buckshot.

The old man and his sons scrambled behind their truck.

Morgan began walking toward them, firing, his pistol extended in a two-handed grip. He walked forward in a crouch, keeping his upper body still as his knees acted as shock absorbers.

He knew that, on his right, Virgil was also walking forward, firing the shotgun. Morgan emptied his pistol and combat-loaded another magazine. He had unconsciously brought the weapon in front of his chest while simultaneously dropping the empty magazine to the ground. He drew out a full magazine with his left hand, put the tip of his index finger on the first round, inserted the magazine, and jammed it home with his left palm. He then rolled his left hand over the .45, grasped the slide, pushed his right hand forward, and continued firing as he walked.

People watching from the Grill later said that the reload had been so fast he did not even break stride.

By this time, Morgan knew instinctively that Virgil had fired seven rounds and was now reloading while he continued to walk and fire. Morgan was nearing the corner of the truck front when the old man began to holler to stop firing.

Morgan told him and his sons to slide their weapons to the back of the truck and to back toward him with their hands behind their heads. By this time, Virgil had come around the rear of the truck and was aiming the shotgun at the old man and his sons.

Only the old man backed from behind the truck. Morgan hollered, "Virgil?"

"Both the boys are down with wounds to the head and upper body. Here are their weapons."

Virgil kicked their weapons to the front of the truck as he positioned himself so he could cover both the old man and his sons with the shotgun. His eyes continually shifted between the Wilsons and the surrounding area while he dialed the emergency number on his cell phone.

Morgan holstered his pistol, went to the old man, and told him to get on his knees with his hands interlaced behind his head. He then handcuffed the old man and placed him face down on the ground. He searched him but found nothing.

Morgan went to Jason, put his fingers on his neck, and could feel a slight pulse. As he got back up, he muttered, "Dammit," to himself and quickly went to examine the other two Wilson boys, who still lay bleeding behind the truck.

One of them had several holes in his head from buckshot and was bleeding profusely. Morgan did the best he could to stop the bleeding by using the boy's jacket and belt to tie a pressure bandage around his head.

The third son was rolling and moaning when Morgan reached him. Morgan quickly searched him for any additional weapons and found none. The wounds on the boy's head were not serious, but he had a sucking chest wound that was bubbling air. Morgan pulled off the boy's belt and jacket, folded the jacket, put it on the wound, and tightened the belt around his chest.

He then rose and went to examine the county supervisor's wound. Virgil still stood guard with the shotgun in one hand while continuing to talk on the cell phone.

Morgan knelt beside Thacker, who seemed to be hyperventilating. Morgan tried to calm him as he examined him for wounds. The county supervisor had been hit in the left arm but was not seriously wounded. Morgan took off Thacker's suit jacket, tied it around his arm, and told him to keep pressure on the wound.

By this time he could hear the sirens in the distance. He needed to call both the sheriff and the judge. When they were alone, he intended to ask the judge why the old man was so angry that he had gone to that extreme. He felt it was unusual that Wilson's tax complaint had not already been resolved because the judge normally knew about these issues and smoothed them over.

"Dammit," he muttered again. He hated shooting his own people instead of protecting them.

CHAPTER 5

THE CRIME SCENE

A cell phone was ringing, but Morgan couldn't tell which one. Rachel, who always rose early, came into the bedroom and handed him the phone. Morgan mumbled something but was not quite sure what it was. He listened to the dispatcher and instantly came awake, saying, "OK, I'll be there in about thirty minutes."

He turned to Rachel, who was sitting on the edge of the bed. "Virgil just found a body at the drill site on Thornton Mountain."

He was now fully recovered from his last tour in Afghanistan. Rachel had finally cured his restlessness at night, and his wounds were completely healed. And he was now the chief deputy sheriff for the county.

He took his coffee, walked into the bathroom, and began to strop his straight razor in preparation for shaving. He was old-fashioned about some things, and shaving was one of them. The truth was, he was old-fashioned about a lot of things but did not seem to recognize it. The straight razor just felt better on his face than a safety razor.

Because it was still early, Rachel had not left for work and was making coffee and toast that he could take with him. Morgan knew how busy she was and always appreciated the small things she did for him. She knew that and always found time to please him.

When he arrived at the drilling location, Virgil was already there and had already put up crime scene tape and was taking pictures. Only three workers and Virgil were present. As Morgan got out of the truck with his coffee, Virgil came over to him. Morgan handed him a cup of coffee that Rachel had made for him. Virgil knew where it came from and nodded his thanks.

"What do you have, Virgil?"

Virgil began his description of the events. He said the foreman of the drilling crew had arrived on the drill site around 0530 and discovered the body. He had not touched anything but had immediately called the dispatcher, who had notified Virgil. When he arrived at the site, he had briefly examined the dead body and had then asked the dispatcher to call Morgan.

In the meantime, he had taken numerous pictures with the digital camera each deputy carried in his cruiser. He ended his summary by saying, "The crime scene is still virgin."

Morgan started chuckling. Virgil grinned and said, "This job is ruining my language."

"Any footprints or tire marks?" asked Morgan.

"None that I can find directly related to the body."

Morgan told him to keep the investigative notes and the evidence log. Then he raised the tape and walked toward the body, which lay on its stomach. He drew latex gloves from his jacket pocket and pulled them on. He could see that the feet had been taped together and the hands taped behind the back. He squatted and searched the body for identification.

He muttered to Virgil, "His name is Tim Mullen." He looked through the rest of the wallet and passed it to Virgil for logging. Next he examined the watch and ring. He showed the inscription inside the ring to Virgil as he handed it to him. He then began his physical examination, with Virgil taking notes of his comments. There were no immediate signs of trauma on the back, so Morgan pulled his knife, tripped the blade, and cut the tape binding the hands and feet.

He then asked Virgil to help him turn the body and to keep taking pictures and notes.

One of the drillers standing behind the crime tape asked him if he was going to wait until forensics had processed the scene.

Morgan looked at the man, did not recognize him, and assumed he was from out of the state and had been watching too much CSI. He simply stated, "I also work forensics."

It was a small county with so few murders that they did not have a forensics team. If that really became necessary, they called the state police. Logan County had its share of killings, but they were mostly disputes between relatives or friends. The survivor normally called or came to the sheriff's office to explain how and why the killing had happened.

After the body had been rolled, Morgan again saw no evidence of blunt trauma, no bullet holes, no knife wounds, not even scratches. He sat back on his heels and continued to look at the body.

He suddenly leaned forward and raised one of the dead man's eyelids, closed it, then raised the other one. He again sat back on his heels, muttering an oath.

He looked at Virgil and motioned him down. He then raised one eyelid and then the other. Virgil squatted beside him.

Morgan examined between the body's fingers and under the nails for a needle mark. He then went to the left foot and started to take off the shoe. He felt Virgil's hand on his shoulder and looked at him. Virgil said softly, "Look at the navel."

Morgan nodded and began to unbutton the shirt. Virgil was shining a light on the navel in order for Morgan to better examine it. Inside the navel and barely visible was a small needle mark.

Morgan pulled the shirt down, and both men rose to their feet. They looked at one another. This killing technique was used by selected special operations teams, and they had seen it used several times in Afghanistan. *Hell*, thought Morgan, *we even used the technique ourselves.*

He told Virgil to get the EMTs to pick up the body and take it to the hospital prior to shipping it to Frankfort for an official autopsy.

The sheriff had arrived while Morgan was examining the body. Over the last several months, the sheriff had begun to move more and more things off his desk onto Morgan's and to give him more freedom in running the department. He stood beside his four-wheel-drive truck, talking to the drill foreman and drinking his morning coffee.

Morgan raised the crime tape and walked toward him.

"Morgan," said the sheriff, nodding good-morning.

Morgan nodded to the sheriff and the drill foreman. The sheriff leaned his head to the left, indicating they should talk in private. He walked several yards away, and Morgan followed him. The people present at the site edged away, giving them privacy.

The sheriff silently handed Morgan the other cup of coffee he was holding and said, "It's black." Morgan nodded his appreciation, took a sip, and began to brief him.

The victim's name was Tim Mullen of St. Paul, a town about thirty miles to the east. It was a professional hit, most likely by a former Special Forces operative. He had subdued the victim, most likely with a weapon, then blindfolded him and taped his hands and feet. There did not appear to be any struggle, so the shooter had been very sympathetic to the victim in an attempt to calm him and get him to relax. The shooter had then drugged the victim with a needle to the navel. When the victim was unconscious, the shooter had raised each eyelid and, with a silenced .22, put a subsonic round into each eye, then closed the eyelids.

The sheriff looked at the EMTs loading the body into the ambulance and asked, "No forensics?"

Morgan replied, "There will be no evidence. This guy is a professional."

Virgil came up to where they were talking and asked about his coffee. The sheriff looked at him and replied, "Virgil, you are a lowly sergeant in the department, and the sheriff does not get sergeants their coffee. The sergeants get the sheriff his coffee."

He continued to verbally abuse Virgil, which he had been doing since Virgil was a boy. "Apparently your training officer is not doing his job properly. By the way, who was your training officer?"

Vigil looked at Morgan. "I might have known," said the sheriff. "Neither of you has any respect for the chain of command in this department." Then he ordered, "Virgil, go manage the crowd."

Virgil looked at the three people at the crime scene and replied as the sheriff suspected he would: "But there are only three people."

The sheriff looked at him and said, "Virgil, in this county, three people are a crowd. Now go manage the crowd."

Virgil walked toward the crowd, shaking his head.

The sheriff smiled. "There are times when I love this job." He nodded for Morgan to continue.

Morgan laughed slightly and continued his analysis. The victim had been murdered somewhere else. He was most likely laid onto a plastic sheet then killed. He was then wrapped in the plastic sheet, transported to this location in a truck, and then dumped where he'd be found by the drill crew.

Morgan explained to the sheriff that this was not a random dump but most likely a warning to the drilling company, a warning to the environmental group protesting the drilling, or a warning to someone else or perhaps some other group. "It is a warning to someone, anyway. If this was someone from this area they would normally drop the body into a mine shaft or have the hogs dispose of it. Once we know who is being warned, we can establish a motive."

The sheriff looked out over the mountains and asked, "Anything else?"

"I don't like the feel of it. I'll do the leg work to eliminate the drill company and the environmentalists, but I think this thing may lead us where we may not want to go."

The sheriff shrugged and said, "I think it will get right interesting. Just follow it anywhere it leads." With that he got into his truck and left.

CHAPTER 6

GRANDMA

A week later, Rachel looked at Morgan one morning and said, "Morgan, you have been home awhile now. I think it's time you visited your grandmother." Rachel felt strongly about taking care of his relatives and visited his grandmother about every two weeks.

Morgan knew she was right and told her they would visit her on Sunday. He thought it would be good to visit his grandmother again. She seemed to act as a personal post office for that part of the mountains, so in addition to the visit, he would also discuss the murder with her.

A lot had happened since he had stepped off the bus and they had begun living in the new house rather than the trailer. As chief deputy for the county, he had been working the county every day, networking with people who informed him of county criminal enterprises, mostly dealing with moonshine or meth. Unless the moonshining got out of hand, both he and the sheriff viewed it simply as local family businesses, since in many cases it had been going on for over two hundred years.

Morgan had regained twenty pounds and was exercising daily at the new county Recreation Center. The county was proud of it, for it compared favorably with those found in the surrounding counties. The judge had decided to build the new facility, intending to be proactive to protect the health of the county people. Morgan liked the idea of preventive health care, especially for the mountain people, and thought the rest of the state should adopt it.

He had also continued to practice with the .45, spending at least fifteen minutes a day with the weapon before reporting for duty. In addition, he was meeting with Virgil at least once a week and steadily improving his speed and precision through the numerous drills they had perfected while in the military. If anything, he thought he was faster than when he had left for his last tour in Afghanistan. The gunfight at the Mountain Grill had certainly proved the necessity of constant practice.

On Sunday, Rachel had Morgan load a large backpack into the truck, which contained groceries for his grandmother and a large amount of medicine. In addition, she had packed a smaller bag containing her medical kit. It was about a two-hour drive to his grandmother's cabin. It wasn't that far in a straight line, but with the dirt roads, winding mountain curves, and a four-mile walk it took almost two hours.

His grandma used to live near where their new house was. But in the late 1940s, when his grandfather had not returned from the war, she had moved back to the cabin where she had grown up. She had taken her family with her, and that is where he was born and spent several years while his father was in Vietnam. *Hell,* he thought, *the truth is the Morgans liked to fight and everyone knows it. All of us seem to run out of the mountains at the first opportunity, looking for a war.*

They parked next to the creek in front of Jed Lafferty's house. It had a railing fence around it and was weather-beaten and patched in several places. Chickens were scratching in the front yard. Jed's wife came out to the path next to the creek and spent several minutes discussing her health with Rachel. Rachel liked the mountain people, and they, in turn, liked her.

Because of their isolation, the mountain people were difficult to get to know, but she and Morgan had been raised in the mountains and were accepted. If the mountain people knew a person's parents and grandparents, then they were generally accepting. If not, then that person was a stranger, an outsider, and not to be trusted. Morgan knew that made for strong family loyalties, which he valued above all else. He also knew that when he fought, it was for his family or the people around him.

The truth was, sometimes he fought just because he felt good. And he felt good a lot. He did not know it, but he was smiling and laughing to himself.

Jed's wife looked at Rachel and said, "Morgan entertaining himself again?" Rachel looked at him, nodded, and continued the conversation.

They walked about two miles up the mountain path, which was a walking path no wider than a horse. The mountains were green once more. It had been a hard winter, and the trees were glad to see the sun. A hundred yards ahead, the path passed through a small glade of trees. An Indian stood in the path. When they reached him, Rachel was in front and Morgan was two paces behind and to her right.

Ignoring Morgan, Tom Cold Moon began to talk to Rachel in Cherokee.

"*Si yo Dto hi tsu.*"

"*Si da ni hi na*?"

After their initial greeting, their conversation continued about the next council meeting. Morgan could struggle through the language, but Rachel had learned it as a child. For Tom, Morgan did not exist. He was simply Rachel's protector and had no more importance than her accompanying tame wolf.

It had been like this from the first day Morgan's father had served as an escort for Rachel's mother. Morgan had been about twelve years old when his father had brought him, Rachel, and her mother to visit Morgan's grandmother. His mother had died the previous summer, and Rachel's mother had insisted that Morgan was old enough to accompany them. When they had encountered an Indian at that very location, only Rachel and her mother had talked to the Indian. Morgan and his father stood in back of them and were ignored.

Morgan also remembered being with his father when they had accompanied Rachel and her mother to a council meeting. The Cherokee had a longhouse especially built for the council meeting. The council members sat in chairs around a fire. Behind them sat their advisers, who were the elderly women of the tribe. Behind the chief sat Rachel and her mother—Rachel on the chief's left and her mother on his right. They were dressed alike and could be taken for Indians with their dark, braided hair. But they had violet eyes that seemed to flash in the firelight. Rachel's mother would occasionally bend forward, as the other women did, and whisper advice into the chief's ear.

These were images that still stuck with Morgan as he waited for the conversation to end. His father had told him that as Rachel's mother got older, Rachel would be on the chief's right and her daughter would be on his left. At that time, he asked his father why they escorted the Leandro women. He shrugged and said it had always been thus. He knew his father, grandfather, and great-grandfather had always accompanied the Leandro women. He thought it somehow might go back to when a Morgan accompanied a Leandro woman through the Cumberland Gap but was not sure.

Morgan had once asked Rachel how she was related to the tribe. She had quietly explained that in the 1830s, the Indians had refused to move when President Jackson had ordered their removal to the Oklahoma territory. Instead, many had fled to eastern Kentucky and settled on and around this mountain, where the Leandro women lived, and sought their protection. Rachel had made it clear that she considered the removal of the Cherokee nothing short of cultural genocide. He knew there was more to the relationship, but when he had asked her, she had put her hand on his cheek and whispered in his ear,

"It is Leandro women's business and only for them." It had always been this way, so he had accepted it.

Grandma was waiting on the cabin porch for them as they came around the last bend in the path. She was dressed as usual in a long, black dress with her hair in a bun at the back of her neck. Even at ninety, you could tell she had been a beautiful woman.

The sheriff had once said the Morgan boys always seemed to marry above themselves, considering they were fighting men and not much good for anything else. Morgan figured that was about right.

The cabin was sitting on stilts. It had a front porch containing a rocking chair and a short bench along the wall. On the end of the porch stood a barrel of smoked apples covered with a quilt. To the left of the cabin stood a silver maple tree, while a rock chimney, built by his great grandfather, was on the right side of the cabin. Next to that cabin was a mountain stream that his grandma used for water. She stood on the porch with her right hand shading her eyes and her left hand on her hip.

Morgan walked up the steps and hugged his grandmother. She stood back and looked up at him. "Well," she said, "it's about time you came to visit me. I see Rachel is taking good care of you and has removed some of that restlessness. Are you fully recovered now?" He nodded and hugged her again.

"Come on in, boy," she said. "I've got some coffee and apple pie waiting for you."

They went through the cabin into the kitchen. The cabin had only two rooms. In the living room was a fireplace and one bed. Along one wall stood long shelves of books, many in French and German. Next to the door into the kitchen was a medicine cabinet where his grandmother kept her medicine. She turned to Rachel, winked, and asked, "Did you bring my medicine?"

Rachel replied, "Yes, I did, Grandma," and put several clear bottles of liquid in the cabinet. As his grandmother passed between the rooms, she always stopped at the cabinet and took a drink of her medicine. And by midafternoon, she was always feeling better. Her family—and she had a large family—always made sure she was never without her medicine. They always joked about it, but never in her presence.

The kitchen was small and consisted of a long table with two benches on each side. On the other side of the kitchen was an antique wood burning stove. Behind the stove was a freshly chopped pile of logs. The room had two windows, one next to the table and one next to the stove.

As they sat at the table, drinking coffee, Morgan told his grandmother about the war, the Afghan tribes and people, the men from the mountains he had served with, his wounds, the time at the veterans' hospital in Lexington, and his new job as chief deputy. As he talked, he became less reserved and more excited, as if he had never left the cabin. His grandmother and Rachel were both good listeners and encouraged him with their questions.

By the time he had finished, he had eaten half a pie and drank three cups of coffee. He realized he felt a lot better. He said, "I'm currently investigating the murder on Thornton Mountain. Do the people you talk to happen to know anything about it?" He did not expect a direct answer and didn't get one.

"When was the last time you were over in Beech County and talked to Sheriff Bailey?" she asked.

"He is on my list of people to visit," he replied.

She merely nodded, picked up his plate and cup, and put them in a dishwashing pan on the stove. She patted his shoulder and simply said, "You did good, son; you did good. Your grandpa and daddy would be proud of you." He knew that was true and felt even better.

She turned to Rachel and said, "They will be arriving soon."

Morgan got up from the table, went outside, and put several benches in the shade along the cabin wall. Rachel unpacked her medicine, put everything on the table, and sat down with his grandma to get the mountain news.

Morgan walked around the outside of the cabin to the front porch and sat on the bench against the cabin wall. He closed his eyes, leaned back against the warm cabin logs, and enjoyed the warmth of the afternoon sun. It was good to be home.

Tom Cold Moon came around the side of the cabin and joined Morgan on the bench. They shook hands as if they had not seen each other that day. Tom Moon, his white name, was a lawyer in the next county and like all the Indians had learned to assimilate into the mountain culture while still retaining his own.

They sat enjoying the sun and idly talking about events in the hills, while the mountain women with their children were being examined and treated by Rachel on the other side of the cabin.

CHAPTER 7

THE COEBURN BOYS

He drove the truck slowly up to the house at the end of the dirt road. When he arrived, he called out the window, "Aunt Minnie, can I get down and come in?"

He knew he could, but with Aunt Minnie, it paid to be courteous. He had learned a lot about dealing with mountain people from observing his father.

Aunt Minnie came to the door and saw who it was. "Morgan, I've been expecting you. Get down and come in. I've got coffee and apple pie on the table for you."

He smiled, remembering the times he had gone there with his mother and father to visit with his cousins, the Coeburn boys.

The last time he had seen his aunt had been just before he, Virgil, and Ancil departed for Afghanistan. She was a tall, slim woman who liked her solitary ways and didn't mind her own company. She sat in the other room in a chair next to the door while he sat at the table eating his pie and drinking coffee. Since the fire, no one had seen her face but everyone respected her desire to be left alone. She, like all Morgan women, had been good-looking and a little conceited about her looks.

They made small talk as he asked how she was doing, and she asked about Rachel and the clinic. She had heard they had expanded again.

Rachel had visited her regularly and respected her wishes, as Aunt Minnie knew she would. Rachel had never even talked to Morgan about it. He had asked her one time and had gotten "that look," so he had quickly backed off and never asked again.

Morgan asked her about Denver and Mason. She said she had seen all the boys that morning when Virgil had come for a visit, but when they heard Morgan was coming they had decided to walk down the hill to meet him. She didn't understand why he hadn't seen them. Morgan smiled and started to feel good. But then he always seemed to feel good around the Coeburn boys.

"Aunt Minnie, have you heard about the killing over on Thornton Mountain?"

"Just that it was that Mullen man from St. Paul. My neighbors don't seem to know what it was about or who did it. One mentioned that he thought he was some sort of transporter, since he made regular trips out of state."

"Did they give any idea of what he might be transporting?"

"They didn't know but thought it might be meth or bath salts. The women who told me this had heard he may be involved in transporting more than meth but didn't say what."

Morgan thanked her and got up to leave. "Aunt Minnie, tell the boys I stopped by."

As he went out the door, he said, "Call me if you need me for anything." He got back into the truck, waved toward the door, and started back down the mountain.

Morgan was careful as he drove; he needed to be constantly alert for deer, bear, or elk crossing the dirt road. As he rounded a curve, he spotted Denver and Mason standing in the middle of the road. Virgil sat on a log at the side of the road.

Morgan laughed with pleasure, for he knew what was about to happen. *Damn, it's good to be young, feel good, and have cousins.*

Denver was the oldest, biggest, and slyest. He seemed to like nothing better than a fight, and it didn't seem to matter who it was with. Morgan had once seen him walk up to a total stranger and hit him for no reason. Mason was the middle one—a little more cautious than Denver but not by much. Virgil was the youngest and most thoughtful. He had only been a couple years behind Morgan in school. They had played basketball together. Virgil had saved his life in Afghanistan, and Morgan felt closest to him of all his cousins, and there was a bunch of them running around the hills with their hair on fire. He smiled at the thought.

Virgil cringed when he saw Morgan smile, for he knew what was about to happen. He always had that smile when he was about to enjoy himself, and he always seemed to enjoy himself around the Coeburn boys.

As Morgan exited the truck, he said, "Howdy, boys. Nice day. Now get the hell out of the road before I whip all three of you."

The Coeburn boys started to laugh, for it was a nice day, and they were all going to enjoy themselves.

Virgil spoke first. "Boys, two on one might be a little unfair."

Morgan grinned and said, "Well, knuckleheads, I agree that it's not fair. Virgil, you want to join your brothers to even the odds?"

"Well, if you enjoy yourself too much with these two, I may have to join the fun," Virgil replied.

Denver motioned Mason to a log beside of the road. Mason walked to the side of the road, reached behind the log, pulled out a quart of moonshine, unscrewed the cap, and took sip before handing it to Virgil.

Virgil took a sip and looked questioningly at Morgan, who took the quart jar from Virgil's hand and took a sip.

He looked at Virgil. "Tastes like old lady Combs's moon." Virgil nodded, indicating he had surmised correctly.

Just then a left hand hit Morgan in the stomach, and he went flying across the road. All three of the Coeburn boys laughed as Morgan lay at the edge of the road, retching up the moonshine.

Morgan looked calmly at Denver and said, "I'm going to break your left arm for that." Morgan and the Coeburn boys liked to fight each other and their other cousins fairly, but outside the family, it was a back-alley brawl that could turn deadly.

He picked up his hat, took off his gun belt, walked to the truck, and placed them both in the front cab. He then walked back toward Denver, who was quick on his feet. Denver quickly jabbed with his left and crossed with the right.

Morgan was expecting that move and shifted his head first right then left. Denver's right fist grazed Morgan's right ear. At the same time, Morgan spread his right thumb and forefinger and stuck Denver in the throat with the stretched web. Denver immediately began gagging in an attempt to get his breath. Morgan quickly flicked the back of his right hand into Denver's groin, grabbed his left arm, and did a hip throw. As Denver hit the ground, Morgan straightened his left arm and broke it across his knee. Denver began to squall and roll on the ground.

As Denver rolled in pain, Mason got off the log and ran at Morgan.

Virgil, continuing to sit on the log, hollered, "Big mistake, Mason."

Morgan rolled to his left and swept his right leg across the back of Mason's legs as he started to stomp him. When Mason went to the ground, Morgan raised his right leg and smashed his heel into Mason's groin. He then rolled to the right and came to his feet.

Virgil was still sitting on the log with the jar of moonshine in his hand. He slowly set the jar down, looked at Morgan, and said with a laugh, "You know, Morgan, I'm going to have to have a go at you."

Morgan laughed. "I'd expect nothing less, Virgil."

They met in the middle of the road, both arms raised, elbows close to their ribs with their hands in a knife edge. Virgil quickly went sideways and snapped a kick to Morgan's left knee in an attempt to disable it. Morgan pivoted on his right toe, planted his left foot, and snapped a kick toward Virgil's right knee. Neither kick connected, so they both circled. By this time, both Denver and Mason had crawled out of the road and were lying next to the log, each taking sips from the moonshine jar and watching the show.

Morgan realized that Denver had started the fight just to get Morgan and Virgil into it. He took a step back and laughed as he realized he had been manipulated by Denver. He thought, *Denver may be dumb as a coal bucket, but he's a devious bastard.*

Virgil reached to the ground, picked up a handful of gravel and dust, and quickly tossed it underhand toward Morgan's face and eyes. Virgil followed quickly, but Morgan went to the ground on his left side, hooked his left foot around Virgil's left ankle, and kicked Virgil's left thigh with his right foot. When Virgil went to the ground, Morgan kicked him in the ribs with his right heel, and the fight was over.

Virgil rolled on the ground, attempting to get his breath. When he did, he said, "Damn, Morgan, for a minute there I thought you were going to break my leg."

"No such luck, Virgil. I need you."

Morgan got slowly to his feet and walked over to Denver, who handed him the jar of moonshine with his right hand. Morgan took a swallow and looked at the jar. "I swear, boys, I don't know how you drink this stuff." He took another sip.

Morgan put a splint on Denver's arm and taped Virgil's ribs with duct tape. He put all three in the truck and told them he would take them to Rachel's clinic for proper treatment.

As he neared the truck, he turned and spoke to the woods. "Aunt Minnie, the boys are all right. Virgil has a possible broken rib, Denver a broken arm, and Mason was just embarrassed. I'm going to take them to Rachel's for proper medical care. After that, I'll bring them back home."

From the woods, he heard Aunt Minnie laugh. "Morgan, I do think you have a mean streak wider than both your daddy and granddaddy put together."

He laughed as he got in the truck, where the Coeburn boys were still passing the jar. He thought it had been a nice day. After all, they all had enjoyed themselves.

Virgil passed the jar to Morgan, who took a sip and, in turn, passed it to Denver in the back seat. Morgan put the truck in gear and started down the mountain.

CHAPTER 8

THE CLINIC

Morgan pulled onto the emergency parking ramp and honked his horn. Rachel and two medical technicians came running out of the emergency ward, anticipating a major injury. They stopped when the Coeburn boys stumbled out of the truck.

Rachel looked at Morgan and said accusingly, "They are drunk again, and you have been fighting! Morgan, you have *not* fully recovered."

Morgan slowly nodded, for he knew she had a temper, and said, "The boys are not badly hurt. I only banged them up a little. Virgil has a possible broken rib, Denver has a broken arm, and Mason is just embarrassed."

The Coeburn boys tipped their hat to Rachel as they always did when talking to her. They had shown the same respect toward her in childhood.

Virgil spoke up. "Rachel, I think he's fully recovered. He didn't even break a sweat this time."

She quickly looked them over. "Well, maybe, except you boys never could fight very well."

They had always been unarmed against her verbal assaults and simply nodded and kept quiet.

She quickly triaged their injury and said she would see Virgil first. All four men walked into the emergency ward, which was not busy at the time.

Rachel examined Virgil and ordered an X-ray to make sure the rib had not punctured a lung. Virgil left with one of the technicians. She was good-looking, and Virgil smiled at his brothers as he followed her down the corridor.

Rachel saw Virgil's smile. "Virgil, no funny stuff in the lab, or I will make life miserable for you."

Morgan and the remaining Coeburn boys laughed.

As they waited for Virgil to return from the X-ray lab, Morgan and Mason could hear her examine Denver, who kept complaining about his arm. "Denver, quit whining," she said. "You are so drunk you cannot possibly feel any pain." She continued her verbal assault on him, and he sat there meekly.

All the Coeburn boys seemed to enjoy it when she quarreled at them. She informed Denver that she knew he was the sly one and had somehow maneuvered Morgan into the fight and that he should be ashamed of himself. She picked up one of the largest needles in the lab, pointed it at Denver, and began threatening him with all sorts of dire consequences.

Mason looked a Morgan. "She sure has a sharp tongue."

Morgan grinned and said, "Tell me about it."

"Morgan, I heard that. Now wipe that grin of your face, or I'll use this needle on you." Both Denver and Mason started cackling.

After being treated for their injuries, Morgan and the Coeburn boys were outside getting ready to drive back up the mountain. Rachel came through the door and gave each of the Coeburn boys a hug and a kiss on the cheek and told them she wanted no more nonsense. She also informed them that she had talked to Aunt Minnie, and they would also hear from her at supper.

She suddenly started laughing and said, "I wish I'd seen that fight. Looks like you did enjoy yourselves."

Morgan and Coeburn boys just grinned, got in the truck, and drove toward the mountain.

CHAPTER 9

SALLIE CONLEY

d ays after the fight with his cousins, Morgan began to think once more about how best to implement the changes he had described to the sheriff. One evening over the dinner table, he brought the conversation around to the changes he wanted to implement, described the changes to Rachel, and explained his rationale for each one. He also told her about the three people he wanted to recruit. "What do you think?" he asked.

She went to the heart of the changes. "Morgan, I'm not going to tell you things you haven't already thought of, so bear with me." He had always valued her insight into personnel issues and listened attentively.

After dinner, he went to the porch overlooking the bluish gray mountains, listened to "La Vie En Rose" by

Chet Atkins, and rethought his plans for implementing the changes. As he sat, the sun formed a red haze above the mountaintops. The clouds became a fiery barrier against the night sky, while the fog drove the shadows from the valley floor. He was home and felt at peace.

What had she said? he mused. *The process is the product.* He knew that sometimes in his haste to accomplish a mission, he overlooked the human cost of the mission or the change process. He also knew from his military experience that too many rapid changes would be resisted. They had to come at just the right pace and show immediate results to be truly accepted by the people in the organization. In addition, the changes had to be institutionalized over time to be effective. He was looking forward to the challenge.

Hell, he thought, *fifty percent of the deputies are going to be unhappy with any decision, while the other fifty percent will watch the fun.* He sat there laughing, while Rachel simply shook her head. She had married a crazy man, and everyone knew it.

The next day he began to meet with each deputy and discuss with them the changes he intended to make. The majority realized the proposed changes would benefit the department. Several questioned the necessity of many of the changes, but after Morgan had explained his rationale, they readily acknowledged the benefit.

Three of the deputies were old even when Morgan had been hired as a new deputy. All three said they were too old to make the changes and intended to retire. Morgan had expected this. But these were experienced men who were liked and respected by the county's citizens, and

Morgan did not want to lose them. So he offered to bring them back into staff positions after they retired.

After discussing it with Mable, he decided to hire them as her staff assistants. He asked her to plan an elaborate retirement ceremony for them, to be held on the steps of the courthouse.

He also had previously signed a contract with Ancil to perform "special duties" to be assigned by himself, the sheriff, or the judge. So he now had three vacancies to fill and knew the people he wanted—if he could convince them.

The first on his list was Sallie Conley. He called and talked to her mother, who told him she was visiting her grandmother to cut wood for the winter.

He drove up the winding dirt road leading up the hollow and stopped behind her car, which was parked at a wide place in the road. He got out of the truck and walked up the path to the house. It was a fading, weathered house standing on stilts that had seen better days, but contained good memories, and he had been part of many of them.

A mangy hound dog lying in the shade of the porch looked up, recognized him, and laid his head down again. As many times as he had been there, Morgan had never seen the dog move from that position.

Sallie was at a chopping block in back of the house. Morgan stood patiently for several minutes at the corner of the house, watching her work. She swung the ax with grace and skill, letting the weight of the ax head do the work of splitting the wood. *A soft mountain woman made of rawhide and whalebone,* he thought. She was a tall, slim muscular woman who didn't mind fighting. He knew from experience that when the tall winds blew, she would stand firm.

When Sallie became conscience of his presence, she embedded the ax in the chopping block and walked toward him. "Captain, I didn't hear you come up." She had a soft mountain lilt that Morgan enjoyed.

"No longer captain, Sallie. Just Morgan."

"Grandma's got some coffee on. Do you want some?" she asked then grinned. "But you always do."

Grandma Conley hugged him and told him he was looking good considering the war. Morgan smiled and swung her around as his father used to do. She laughed and said that Sallie's mother had called, and Paul Burton, who had the only telephone in the hollow, had stopped by and told them he was coming.

Grandma Conley said, "Now you two sit here on the porch, and I'll get some coffee."

They sat on the front steps, looking down the hollow.

"You doing OK now, Morgan? I heard that grenade ripped you up pretty good."

He pulled her close and kissed her on her cheek. "Yeah, Virgil pulled me out of the house and stopped the bleeding. You know how Virgil can get at times, so he called in a gunship and leveled the place."

Sallie had been with the military police near where Morgan and his Shooters were posted. She had visited regularly to practice with them. Morgan thought she was a natural with a pistol and almost the equal of either of them. She had later proved it by cleaning out a ditch line of Taliban waiting to ambush a convoy. She had run down the ditch line, killing everyone she encountered. Morgan,

Virgil, and Ancil had made it a point to attend the ceremony where she was awarded the Silver Star. She had returned early from her last tour because she had lost her husband in a car crash.

"How you doing, Sallie?" Morgan asked.

"Bad day by bad day, Morgan. You did not come up here for small talk. That's not your style."

"Sal, I want you to come work for me as a deputy sheriff." When she noticed he'd shortened her name, she looked at him; he rarely attempted to turn on the charm. Generally he was all business.

"Morgan, don't sweet-talk me. You need me, don't you?"

"I'm not much good at it, am I?"

"In fact, Morgan, you are terrible at it. Everybody always wondered why a woman like Rachel had anything to do with a dullard like you."

"Dammed if I know, Sallie. I've always wondered the same thing myself."

"I'll come work for you on one condition: no more attempting to sweet talk me. You are so bad, I get a headache just listening to you."

"Damn, Sallie, you drive a hard bargain." They started laughing, just as Grandma Conley came out of the house to refill their cups.

By the time Morgan left, Sallie had agreed to come to the office the next morning to start the paperwork. As he walked back down the hill, he smiled and congratulated himself on how smooth he had been in talking her into working for him.

Sallie and her grandmother looked after him as he walked down the path. "You think he's congratulating himself on his attempt to sweet talk me?" Sallie asked.

Her grandmother laughed gently and said, "Undoubtedly. After all, he's a Morgan."

"It's too bad he couldn't stay for dinner."

"You think he knows Rachel called you last night, Sallie?"

"Not a clue, and it would not make any difference if he did. Rachel seems to have had him spellbound even as a teenager."

Her grandmother laughed. "All the Leandro women seem to take good care of their menfolk. Where is he in such a hurry to go?"

"He's going to attempt to recruit two more deputies, Alonzo Hicks from over on Ball Branch and Randy Gayheart from Piney Fork."

"Is Hicks that big colored boy? He would make a good one. I heard the Gayheart boy was released from the service for being gay."

Sallie was always amazed at how blunt her grandmother could be. "No, he was honorably discharged; otherwise Morgan would not consider him. Randy is rather feminine looking and has that reputation, but I don't get that vibe from him."

"Well," her grandmother concluded, "I hear he has a mean streak, so he may be a good one too."

CHAPTER 10

THE TRAINING FACILITY - DAY

Morgan drove through the gate onto the training facility. The sign beside its gate proclaimed it to be the Logan County Law Enforcement Training Facility. The facility had been completed just a week before, and he was eager to try it out ahead of the grand opening scheduled for the following month.

He thought the judge, Rachel, and the sheriff were pleased with it. The money to build it had come primarily from corporate donors. Morgan knew most of the money to build the facility was a grant from the Leandro Institute, a worldwide, nonprofit educational and health organization. He also knew the institute could easily afford it.

Fifteen of the current deputies were gathered in the shooting house, along with the new deputies he had hired.

Sallie Conley was already a full deputy, while Darrell Hicks and Randy Gayheart were scheduled to attend the Southeast Kentucky Law Enforcement Academy starting the next week. In the meantime, Morgan had assigned them training officers, and they were now riding in a cruiser.

Morgan was met at the door by Sergeant Bailey, one of the retired deputies assigned to run the training facility. Bailey was a former marine who liked guns, and when he handed Morgan a perfect cup of coffee and nodded to him, Morgan knew he was happy with his new assignment.

After speaking briefly to each of the deputies, he nodded to Virgil, who called the room to attention. The men stood at attention in front of their seats. Morgan walked to the front, and Virgil gave the command, "Seats." The men were former military, and Morgan had decided to run the department as a highly trained paramilitary organization. No one objected, for all of them were comfortable in that atmosphere.

He reminded them that in order to protect their relatives and friends, one of the more important skills they had to possess was the use firearms. He indicated that they would be evaluated on their skills with a pistol that day, and those found wanting would be scheduled to train weekly and reevaluated in a month.

The current deputies had been qualifying quarterly and, like all mountain men, felt confident in their ability to shoot. But Morgan cautioned them not to be too confident, for the series of exercises they would be performing were rigorous and would demand the utmost skill and fitness on their part. And the exercises were to run all day and into the night.

As he described each exercise, the deputies began to look at one another. Their expressions said this is something different.

Morgan completed his remarks by reminding them that Sallie was the only female on the force but hopefully not the last. He said that she was the newest member of the force, and most of them would be able to outshoot her. At this, Virgil and Ancil looked questioningly at each other. Morgan added that if they did, they would be excused from having to practice that week.

Most of the men looked at Sallie and smiled. *Sure,* she thought, *sure.*

He finally asked, "Any questions?"

Mike Baxter said, "What about lunch and supper?" He was immediately rewarded with several comments about his eating habits. Most of the men had known him a long time and knew he seemed to always be hungry. Morgan laughed too, but he knew that any soldier or marine soon learned to eat and rest whenever they could.

Morgan smiled at him. "Mike, it will be catered by Will's place." At that they shouted their approval, for his pulled-pork sandwiches were popular in the area.

Morgan finally nodded to Virgil, who again called everyone to attention. When he had left the room, Virgil ordered them to fall outside.

Virgil and Ancil were the designated range officers and ran the exercises while Morgan stood near the ambulance with the emergency medical technicians, drinking coffee. Sgt. Bailey would be the scorer, using a large board visible to everyone.

The first exercise would be a simulated foot chase of four hundred yards, followed by the expenditure of ten rounds on different silhouette targets, followed by a reload and an expenditure of ten more rounds on pop-up metal silhouette targets positioned at different distances, heights, and angles.

Morgan watched as the first group of five lined up for the simulated pursuit. Sallie was on the far left of the line.

Virgil gave the command, and the men quickly out-distanced Sallie for the first one hundred yards. At the two-hundred-yard marker, she was even with them, and at the four-hundred-yard marker, she drew her weapon and began to fire while the next deputy was twenty-five yards behind her. She finished her first clip of ten rounds, reloaded, and began to fire her second clip at the metal pop-up silhouette targets, which dropped monotonously with loud clangs after each shot. She had already holstered her weapon when her closest competitor began to fire.

When Sgt. Bailey posted the scores for the exercise, Virgil and Ancil could hardly suppress their smiles; they had seen this before. The men looked stunned. After several more exercises, they looked at Sallie admiringly and realized they were looking at one of the best they had ever seen. Apparently they needed to improve.

After lunch and one hour of rest, Virgil assembled them once more in the classroom. There Morgan described the exercises for the afternoon. There would be a series of timed exercises related to drawing and firing their weapons at targets placed at different distances, angles, and heights, but all within ten yards. It would require point shooting combined with speed and accuracy. This would be followed by reloads executed with both the left and the right hands. The final exercise would be unorthodox shooting positions.

One of the deputies raised his hand and asked, "Why point shooting?" Then he quoted the maxim "In a fight, front sight." A few of the men nodded.

Morgan acknowledged it as a good question and explained, "There have been a number of studies of gunfights involving law enforcement personnel. The first I am aware of was done by Deputy Commissioner William Fairbairn of the Shanghai Metropolitan Police around 1936. The second was done by the FBI around 1996 or 1997. Both studies had similar findings applicable to about 80 percent of the fights. First, the fights took place at speaking distances, normally five to seven yards. Second, both parties in the fight were moving. And, third, the fights took place at night or in low light, so it was impossible to see the front sight."

He said that firefights were sudden and violent, and humans tend to react instinctively since there is no time to plan or think. He indicated that, over thousands of years, human beings have been conditioned by their exposure to danger to either fight, flee, or remain still in order to survive.

He elaborated further. "Your training must supplement and support your natural survival instincts. If you train against your instincts, you will not react naturally and will lose valuable time—and perhaps your life or the life of your friends. You fight to defend your family and friends.

You train for the survival of your family and friends. You train to fight and win. There is no second-place winner in a gunfight."

Everyone nodded. This they could understand. Morgan smiled and thought he had begun to sound like a revivalist preacher. But this was serious business, since the life of the men and their families depended on their skill.

They continued the exercises into the afternoon, with Sallie developing a commanding lead. She seemed to remain fresh and eager for the next exercise, while the others began to tire. Morgan knew he would have to let them rest before the night exercises, so after supper he encouraged them to relax or sleep for the three hours before the night exercise.

CHAPTER 11

THE TRAINING FACILITY - NIGHT

After dark Virgil once more gathered them in the classroom to hear Morgan describe the night activities. "Tonight the first exercise will evaluate your ability to shoot with and without the flashlight. The target will be running targets at various distances. Many of the targets will have only fleeting exposure. You will use both the old FBI and the new Harris technique with flashlights.

"The final exercise of the night will be the mystery house, or shooting house. For many of you, this may be something new. It is designed to simulate the search of a building. Tonight each of you will only get one run through the mystery house. However, it will be a common future exercise. During your training run through the house, you will go through doors, up and down stairways, and through hallways.

"Along the way you will encounter and be forced to deal with various shooting scenarios. Many will be shoot-no-shoot situations. Your journey through the shooting house will be accompanied by screams, shots, the sounds of people running, the opening and closing of doors, and bodies on the floor. The safety officer, Virgil or Ancil, will follow you through the house to make sure you do not inadvertently endanger yourself. This is a 360-degree shooting house fully enclosed by a high earth berm, so you will be shooting in all directions."

They looked at one another and nodded. All of them knew this was more realistic than punching holes in a target.

When Morgan asked for questions, the one he got from Sallie was unexpected. "Rumor has it we are getting new weapons."

Morgan smiled and nodded. Intelligence and law enforcement organizations are incestuous by nature; there were few if any secrets inside an organization. "Well, the cat is obviously out of the bag. These are things I was going to discuss next week. Yes, the department is going to new weapons. We will be switching from 9 mms to .45 ACPs. In addition, each cruiser will carry an M-4 .223 caliber carbine, and the cruiser of each shift supervisor will carry an M-14 30.06 caliber rifle. A sniper team will also be formed and outfitted with two different rifles: the Barrett .50 caliber and the SR 25 rifle."

He looked at each of them. "All of you remember the fight in Los Angeles where the cops were completely outgunned and had to go to a nearby gun store to get enough firepower. I do not intend for us to be involved in situations where we are outgunned."

Everyone nodded.

When everyone had left after the night exercise, Morgan, Virgil, Ancil, and Sgt. Bailey sat at a table in the shooting house.

"What do you think?" Morgan asked.

Virgil spoke first. "All of them have had good basic training, but, except for Sallie, they are not ready to fight. Against a professional they would not stand a chance."

Ancil tentatively agreed. "They have different skill levels, but they all appear to be coachable and willing to commit to improving their ability to fight. I think that trick with Sallie woke them up."

Sgt. Bailey said, "Even with practice, they will have a hard time reaching her level. She is scary woman. A man would be a fool to get her angry."

They discussed what could be done to improve each deputy's fighting ability. Then Morgan asked Virgil and Ancil to create training exercises for each of them. Ancil would act as their coach during the exercises, with Virgil in relief. They had done the same thing several times before in Afghanistan, when new soldiers had joined their organization, so both were comfortable with the arrangement.

Finally he asked Sgt. Bailey to work with their supervisors on a training schedule.

It had been a long profitable day, and they had enjoyed themselves. As they prepared to leave the facility, Ancil said he would ride with Virgil.

As Morgan drove from the facility, he idly wondered when Ancil was going to learn to drive—at least effectively.

CHAPTER 12

THE ATF MAKES A CALL

Mabel Handshoe knocked on Sheriff Harley's door and announced, "Someone here to see you."

The sheriff nodded, and Mabel stepped aside and returned to her desk.

The man who entered the office was dressed in a dark suit, white shirt, and red tie. He was a little shorter than six feet and solidly built. "Sheriff Harley, I'm Agent Barnes from the ATF Field Office in Louisville." His handshake was firm and businesslike.

Harley motioned Barnes toward a seat. After they were both seated, he looked toward the door, expecting Mable to appear with two coffees. When she did not, the sheriff turned to Barnes and began to reassess his first impression.

After several minutes of small talk about mutual acquaintances, his telephone rang. The sheriff excused himself and picked up the telephone. On the other end, Mable quickly briefed him on Barnes's background.

The sheriff returned to the telephone to it cradle, turned his chair, and asked, "What can I do for you, Agent Barnes?"

"We've gotten word that the Combs Gang is running a moonshine operation in Logan County. Our information indicates they are making and selling several thousands of gallons per month. One batch turned up in DC, which resulted in several individuals going to the emergency ward for alcohol poisoning. We would like your support in raiding and closing down their operation."

Sheriff Harley looked at him questioningly. "The Combs Gang? Could you be more specific?"

For several minutes, Agent Barnes briefed Harley on the intelligence the ATF had pieced together regarding the Combs moonshine operation.

"Who provided this information?" Harley asked. "And has it been independently validated?"

Under Harley's questioning, Barnes had to admit that most of the information had come from their intelligence section in DC and had not been independently validated.

After their conversation, Harley looked at his watch and asked Mable to call Morgan and Virgil at the Mountain Grill and to come see him immediately. He then turned to Agent Barnes and asked him to explain what his reasons were for suspecting that the moonshine was poisonous.

Morgan and Virgil walked into the sheriff's office just as they were finishing their conversation.

Harley introduced everyone and briefed Morgan and Virgil on his discussion with Agent Barnes. He then asked, "Morgan, what can you tell us about Jessie Combs's moonshine operation?"

Morgan glanced at Barnes and then looked at Harley questioningly. When Harley nodded, Morgan replied with a neutral voice, "Well, the Combs Gang consists of Jessie Combs and her two sons. The still on Troublesome Creek is a family operation making about one hundred to two hundred gallons per month, primarily for the family, and has been in operation for about 150 years. They make good moon—not like that rotgut made by the Hinckley crowd in Harlan County. She does have an extended family and is not likely to poison them. Why do you ask the question?"

"Agent Barnes wants to raid and destroy her still."

"It's a bad idea. Why don't I just call her and ask her to come down and talk to you about it."

Agent Barnes sputtered, "A hundred fifty years of continuous operation? You knew about it and let her operate? Look, what she is doing is illegal and dangerous. Let's raid them and put a stop to it."

Harley shook his head and looked at Morgan. "Ask her down to discuss this with me and the judge. See if she can be here at eleven tomorrow."

"She doesn't have a telephone, but Ancil knows them. I'll have him ask her to come down. There is a path that runs from Rosemary's place over the hill to Troublesome."

"Morgan, that's fine, but be sure Ancil knows he is to ask and not force her. You know how Ancil can get."

Barnes interrupted again, "Why not let him force her. She is breaking the law."

The sheriff looked at him like he was crazy. "She has two boys that are squirrely in the head, and to threaten their mother would only ask for trouble. This can be resolved without trouble."

"Agent Barnes, have you ever been in the military?" Morgan asked.

"What does that have to do with this situation?"

"There are some military organizations that practice the philosophy of knowing your enemy before getting involved with them. I have served with the Combs boys, and they can be trouble. To rile them unnecessarily would only get someone injured or killed. It is better to ask them neighborly."

The ATF agent again said that they had broken the law and must be stopped.

Morgan looked at him. "There is the law and there is justice, and many times the two are not the same. If you persist in this foolishness, you are going to get someone injured or killed."

Morgan picked up the telephone and dialed his Aunt Rosemary and asked for Ancil. After several minutes of describing her ailments, she finally put Ancil on the phone.

"Ancil, I just put you on the speaker phone, so watch what you say. I want you to go over to Troublesome Creek and ask Jessie Combs to come visit with the sheriff and judge at eleven tomorrow. Make sure she understands that the sheriff would consider it neighborly of her if she would come visit with him. He needs to discuss a complaint that someone has become ill drinking her moon."

"Morgan, that is just plain stupid," Ancil said. "Me and the Coeburn boys drink her moon all the time. Remember that quart jar I brought last time I visited. Well, that came from her still, and you are not dead."

Morgan rolled his eyes and looked at the ceiling. "Ancil, just go tell her. If she needs a ride, let me know, and Virgil will come get her."

After Morgan hung up, the sheriff started laughing and said, "Morgan, you been holding out on me."

The ATF agent looked questioningly at both of them. "This seems highly irregular and a little unprofessional."

Virgil looked at him and said, "Well, she does make good moon. Want a drink?"

The ATF agent snorted, got up, and left. Laughter followed him through the door.

CHAPTER 13

THE COMBS MOONSHINE STILL

The next morning, Morgan was having breakfast with Virgil at the Mountain Grill when he received a call from the dispatcher to see Sheriff Harley immediately.

Morgan looked at Virgil and shrugged. Virgil asked, "You think that ATF agent has done something stupid?"

"Probably."

They quickly finished their breakfast and drove to the sheriff's office. When they arrived, Harley was as angry as Morgan had ever seen him. "Ancil just called," he said, "and told me that the ATF raided the Combs's still early this morning. Two agents are wounded and two are being held prisoner by the Combs boys."

"Morgan, go up there, clean up this mess, and make sure those Combs boys don't kill anyone."

As they left the office, Virgil turned to Morgan and muttered, "Stupid or what?"

Morgan shook his head in disbelief.

He called Ancil and told him to stay with the Combs boys and to make sure the deputies were kept alive until he arrived with Virgil and a doctor. "Now, Ancil, you specifically tell them that Captain Morgan wants those deputies alive and not buried in a mine shaft. Also tell Jessie to meet me at her place."

Morgan then called Rachel and briefed her on the ATF raid and that he would pick her up in about twenty minutes.

Her response: "Now, that was stupid."

Morgan parked beside Jessie Combs's house. In one corner of the yard was a partially dismantled truck. An engine block filled with rainwater was sitting patiently at the edge of the yard. In the middle of the yard was a truck tire painted white with several sunflowers growing out of it. Flying from a large pole was the American flag. In the front window of the house was a gold star.

Jessie was sitting in an old rocker on the front porch waiting for them. She was dressed in breeches that were too large and tightly cinched at the waist with a large, brown belt. She was wearing a plaid shirt, and her gray hair was in a bun at the back of her head.

She rose and nodded to Morgan and Rachel. "Captain Morgan, Rachel, it's good to see you again." She hugged Rachel and shook hands with Morgan while studying Virgil. "Virgil, you still owe me ten dollars for that last quart."

Morgan laughed and looked at Virgil. "Virgil, you been holding out on me."

Jessie described what had happened: "Two deputies are injured, and the other two are trussed up. We had to put a gag in the one with the loud mouth, who acted like the leader.

"The deputies came sneaking through the woods at four o'clock in the morning, when all decent folk should be in bed. They were making enough noise to wake the dead. They tripped the alarms, and the boys went to investigate. Our neighbors know better than to go around stills, so I figured someone wanted to steal my makings.

"The boys were downright polite and told them they did not belong in this area and to leave. But they all of a sudden fired on my boys, who, not wanting to kill them, backed up the hill."

She fairly fumed. "Captain Morgan, any decent, God-fearing peace officer knows to announce themselves at a still. How could these people be so stupid?"

At that pronouncement, Virgil looked at Morgan and grinned.

She continued to describe the incident. The agents had kept advancing until they encountered the booby traps that had been set to protect the still from intruders. "Any *good* peace officer knows that stills have traps. One of the agents stepped on a deadfall, which broke his leg while a second stepped on a pungi stake that went through his boot. The other two agents went to the aid of the injured and were captured without any more trouble."

Rachel indicated she needed to treat the injured, and Jessie led the way to the still. She was not afraid to expose the still's location because they would be moving it.

When they arrived at the still, the two injured deputies were lying about twenty yards from the still site. Their injuries had been treated, and they seemed to be resting comfortably.

The other two had their hands tied behind them, the rope end thrown over a tree limb and their hands raised behind them. Both were blindfolded, but the senior ATF agent also had a taped mouth.

When they saw Morgan, both of the Combs boys stood up and touched their hats. The oldest looked at Morgan and said, "Cap'n, we did what you told us and didn't kill them."

"Boys, you did good. Rachel is going to look after their wounds, so I would appreciate it if you would help her." They nodded and followed Rachel as she checked the wounded.

One of the Combs boys told Rachel they had cleaned the pungi wound with moonshine and then bound the wound tight so it would not bleed. They had then tied a splint on the broken leg to immobilize it. They also had given the agents several cups of moon to combat the pain.

Rachel said to them, "You did fine. Looks like the agents are resting comfortably and appear quite happy, considering their situation.

Virgil saw how the other two agents were tied to the tree and said, "Spanish torture. I haven't seen that since Afghanistan. Hell, the Combs boys are always creative when it comes to tying people up."

Virgil and Ancil lowered the other two ATF agents to the ground and untied them. They removed the blindfolds and the gag from Agent Barnes, who immediately began to yell for Morgan to arrest the two Combs boys. Morgan said, "Shut your mouth, or I'll retape it."

He sent one of the Combs boys back to his truck to get two stretchers. They carried one deputy while Virgil and Ancil carried the other. They were met at the bottom of the hill by an ambulance that transported them and Rachel to the hospital.

Ancil rode with the third deputy back to his lodging while Barnes rode with Morgan and Virgil back to the sheriff's office. When they entered, Harley and Barnes began to shout at each other.

Morgan and Virgil got a cup of coffee and, with amused expressions, silently watched the shouting match. Morgan noticed through the door that Mabel was on the phone. She looked at him and winked. *Probably calling the judge*, he thought.

The judge walked into the room and told them all to shut up and sit down. She then asked Harley to explain what had happened. The judge listened while he explained his actions. He then looked at Morgan, who continued the explanation of events, stressing that the Combs boys had not threatened or fired on the agents and had helped care for their wounds.

Then she asked Barnes to explain what had happened. He explained his actions and his desire to enforce the law. He demanded once more that the Combs Gang be arrested.

The judge replied, "Why didn't you wait for the interview with Jessie at eleven?"

He reiterated, "They were making illegal moonshine, and I needed to take them down in order to prevent any further poisoning."

The judge called the hospital to find out how the deputies were doing. They had been treated but were still drunk. She asked about the results of the moonshine test. The examining chemist said it was some of the best she had examined.

The judge then asked Harley for a sample of the moonshine. He poured a small amount into a glass and handed it to her. She took a sip and looked at him. "She's right. This is good moonshine."

Barnes started to rise from his chair to object. The judge looked at Virgil, who pushed him back into his chair. She then leaned forward in Harley's chair and looked directly at Barnes. "Agent Barnes, you do not come into my county and attempt to arrest my people without my permission. Do you understand that?"

Barnes once again started to object. And once again Virgil pushed him back into the chair.

She looked unsympathetically at Barnes, picked up the telephone, and dialed the number for the Louisville ATF Field Office. When the telephone was answered, she asked for Steve Roper, who was the Special Agent in Charge for that office.

"Steve, this is Judge Leandro in Logan County. Fine, Steve, but I have a problem." She then explained what had occurred and said she could not work with Agent Barnes. "I want another agent to work my county, and I'll handle the Combses."

She handed the phone to the Barnes, who simply said, "Yes, sir…Yes, sir…Immediately, sir," and hung up.

He looked at the judge and said, "My apologies, ma'am. I certainly didn't mean to cause a problem for you." Then he left the office.

CHAPTER 14

BEN WALLACE

Morgan was on his way to discuss the murder on Thornton Mountain with Ben Wallace, the investigative reporter for the *Mountain Herald*. He thought drilling may have played a role in the murder and needed to know more about fracking and the resulting environmental concerns. He had called Ben that morning and told him he needed to talk to him about the murder and how the drilling technology worked. He was not making a lot of progress and was hoping that Ben could provide some leads in the case.

Morgan had lived near Summit City in Logan County all his life but knew very little about the process of extracting gas from deep underground. Ben had written about it for several years, and Morgan figured he was the right person to tell him how the process worked and who might feel strongly enough to kill because of it.

As he passed through Sounding Gap on his way to the *Mountain Herald* office, he noticed a line of white trucks parked alongside the road and recognized them as drilling trucks belonging to the Humboldt company, which operated in that area.

There was heavy truck traffic on the road that morning, and he had already seen at least three heavily loaded coal trucks on their way to the local processing plant near the Virginia border.

The sheriff's dispatcher called and wanted to know if he was near Pine Creek. Morgan replied that he was about a mile from the creek on his way to the *Mountain Herald*. The dispatcher said there was a reported disturbance at the head of the hollow and wanted to know if Morgan would stop by and investigate. Morgan was early for his meeting, so he said he would stop by.

It had been a month since the sheriff's office had responded to a call from that location. He knew it was probably Maude and Delmar Todd again. A disturbance call came out of Pine Creek at least once a month, normally on the third of the month, when the welfare checks arrived at the post office.

He parked his truck at the wide space at the bottom of the hill and started walking a path that separated two hill gardens. Jasper Nelson was leaning on the top rail of a fence, looking toward the Todd house. He had a grin on his face when Morgan stopped and leaned on the fence too.

"You know, Morgan," he said, "this is better than a moving picture show."

"Moving picture show? Jasper, when was the last time you went to a movie? You need to get out of the hollow more often."

"Don't need to, Morgan. All the entertainment I need is right here."

The morning silence was suddenly broken by loud screaming and yelling coming from the Todd house. Morgan knew what was happening and started walking slowly up the dirt path toward the house. He walked slowly to make sure Jasper was properly entertained.

The morning sun had just come over the mountain and was warming the hillside as the morning fog lifted from the hollers and the mountainsides. Morgan was enjoying its warmth on his back and neck when the back door of the Todd house suddenly burst open and Delmar came running out in his white long underwear. Maude came jumping out the back door and ran after him. She was as big and as fast as a mountain lion except she had a kitchen knife in her hand and was swiping at Delmar with every step they took.

As they ran along the path above the gardens, he heard Jasper Nelson whooping and hollering for Maude to fetch him. Fortunately for Delmar, he was faster and was widening the gap between them as he entered the woods.

Morgan finally reached the upper garden path and stood there enjoying the sun and awaiting the results of the chase. He heard Maude in the woods, shouting threats at Delmar. She finally came out of the woods with her gray hair flying in all directions and her torn dress showing her red feedsack petticoat.

As she passed, Morgan stood there grinning and said, "Morning, Maude."

She looked at him as she passed and waved the knife. "Don't say a thing, Morgan!"

Delmar finally poked his head out of the woods and asked Morgan if Maude was back at the house. Morgan replied that she was. Delmar came out of the woods and started discussing his garden with Morgan as if what had happened was normal—which it was.

Delmar indicated he had gotten drunk last night and spent most of the welfare check in a card game and on moonshine. Morgan sympathized with him for a while then walked back down the path to his truck.

He reported the incident to the dispatcher as closed. The dispatcher, who was new to the sheriff's office, wanted to know if he had arrested anyone.

With a laugh, Morgan said, "No, it was just Maude and Delmar Todd enjoying each other's company." He then made a mental note to ask Rachel to check on the Todds' to make sure they had food for the month.

He met Ben Wallace in his office at ten o'clock, and they walked around the corner to the coffee shop to have their discussion. Ben was on the other side of middle age with a middle-age spread. His pants drooped slightly from the bulge at his waist, and he walked with a slight wobble. Morgan knew that he was missing part of one foot from frostbite suffered when the marines retreated from the

Yellow River. His looks were deceiving; Morgan knew that Ben was a tough old bird.

Ben still liked his coffee and cigarettes, even though he was developing a hacking cough. Rachel, who was his doctor, had warned him, but he continued to ignore her advice. It was an ongoing discussion between the two of them, and Morgan had no intention of getting in the middle of it. He knew Ben was not going to change, and he knew Rachel did as well, but it was her job to protect the health of the mountain people, so she persisted. *The truth is*, he thought, *Ben just likes Rachel's attention.*

"Ben, do you know anything about the body on Thornton Mountain?"

Ben looked at him and said, "Nothing but what I read in the newspapers," then attempted to laugh at his joke but only managed to wheeze and cough.

"Ben, that is too old to be funny."

"Well, I thought it was funny. That's the best I can do anymore, and, no, I don't know a thing about the body. I think Sarah Pierce covered that story for the paper, and from what I read she doesn't know a lot either." He once again started his wheezy laugh.

Morgan waited until he had finished wheezing and coughing to tell him he thought it might have something to do with the drilling company. But he was not as informed as he should be, and if he was going to establish any link between the murder and the drilling company, he needed to be more knowledgeable about fracking.

Ben looked at him and asked, "Morgan, what do you know about fracking or, for that matter, mining? And,

Morgan, don't give me any of that dumb hillbilly crap you are so fond of."

Morgan nodded but still confessed his ignorance. "When I was younger, I went down into the mines a couple of times but realized right away that I needed another line of employment. Fracking was after my time, but from what I've heard, it has to do with pumping water into underground rock shale, which breaks the shale. This allows the trapped gas to escape, which can be collected at the surface for processing and distributing. Ben, that truly is about the extent of my knowledge in this area."

Ben took a sip of coffee and said, "The correct term is hydraulic fracturing, which results from the introduction of small explosions through high pressure water to cause the release of shale gas. The explosions, really micro-earthquakes, are caused by the injection of a mixture of water, sand, and chemicals into the rocks. This mixture causes the small explosions that fractures it."

Ben continued. "When a geological survey reveals the presence of shale rock below the surface, normally at about seven to eight thousand feet, a large hole is drilled to a depth of between forty to a hundred and twenty feet, and a large-diameter steel pipe called a conductor casing is installed to stabilize the ground at the top of the well."

Ben took a sip of coffee. "Drilling then continues to a depth below the base of usable water table, typically between a thousand and fifteen hundred feet. At that time, the drill pipe and bit are removed, and a cement sleeve is inserted through a steel casing that is supposed to create a seal that extends from the surface to below the freshwater table."

Ben laughed sarcastically. "And this is supposed to prevent contamination of the drinking water?"

He continued with his explanation. "The drilling continues to around seven thousand feet or until the kickoff point is reached, at which time a special motor is attached to the drill rig, allowing drilling sideways."

"When drilling is stopped, a steel casing is inserted through the entire length of the well, and more cement is pumped through the casing, creating another cement-reinforced container. This casing, running lengthwise, is then perforated, and the water, sand, and chemicals are injected under pressure through the perforation into the shale rock. The sand carried by the mixture is deposited in the narrow fractures, propping them open so gas can flow into the well.

"Each drill site normally uses from about eighty to three hundred tons of water and chemicals with between thirty and fifty percent of the water recovered from the well. The recovered water is highly toxic and must be carefully handled during separation."

Ben took a sip of his coffee and put his cigarette down. After a fit of coughing, he again remarked sarcastically, "Of course that leaves only fifty percent of the toxic water underground."

Morgan liked to talk to Ben, for his biting tongue and pen were well known in the mountains. He asked, "What kind of chemicals are used for fracking?"

Ben replied that by law, fracking companies did not have to disclose the contents of the chemical mixture, but scientists have identified such organic compounds as benzene, toluene, ethylbenzene, and xylene. Morgan decided not to appear more stupid than he already was and to talk to Rachel about those chemicals.

Ben looked at him. "Ask Rachel about the chemicals tonight." Both started laughing. "Those types of chemicals are primarily used in the Marcellus and Utica shale formation in Ohio, Pennsylvania, and New York. In this county, Humboldt uses nitrogen, which is a little safer. After the fracking takes place, the gas is released into the atmosphere, which is already about seventy percent nitrogen."

Ben indicated that opening a well normally took about two to three months, with each well having a productive life of between twenty and thirty years.

Morgan said, "That sounds like a good return on investment, and it might be worth protecting."

Ben looked at him. "Humboldt's income rose from six hundred million dollars to around nine hundred million, primarily due to fracking. There is big money in drilling. Last year alone, gas production brought about twenty-five million dollars in severance taxes back to the state. As you know, the county gets part of that tax."

Ben continued. "It is thought that the carcinogenic chemicals sometimes escape and leak into the water. It is also alleged by environmentalists that the shale gas leaks into the drinking water and sometimes catches fire. There have also been unconfirmed reports of small earthquakes caused by rock fracturing."

Morgan said, "I can see where the environmentalist might get riled up. But if it's dangerous, why isn't fracking illegal?"

Ben explained that in 2005, the Bush/Cheney Energy Bill exempted natural gas drilling from the Safe Drinking Water Act. It also exempted companies from disclosing the chemicals used during hydraulic fracturing. Because of this bill, the Environmental Protection Agency (EPA) had no oversight of fracking. He explained the bill was commonly called the Halliburton Loophole because of Cheney's association with it.

Morgan asked, "Who has a dog in this fight?"

Ben laughed and said, "Now, that is the kind of question your daddy would have asked. You might want to see the tree huggers over at the community college, headed up by Professor Austin. None of them, with the exception of Austin, has the guts to murder anyone. Given Austin's background, he could do it, but I suspect he is simply fronting this as a civics lesson."

Morgan agreed.

Ben continued. "The drilling crew is headed by Paul Allen, but I don't think he had anything to do with the murder, since he takes his orders from the judge, even though he works for Humboldt Drilling. You know the judge likes the gas severance tax to support the county operation, but she is not about to let Allen take any drilling shortcuts.

"You also might want to take a close look at Manners Bolen. I keep hearing rumors he has something going on, but I'm unsure what. He plays things close to the vest, but if the risk is worth it, he is quite capable of ordering a killing or doing it himself."

Ben paused. "But I don't think Manners is involved in this killing. He would be a lot more subtle unless this was intended as a warning. Have you found out anything about the dead man?"

Morgan shook his head. "I'm still in the first stages of the investigation. I know he was from St. Paul and involved in some sort of transportation business, but I have not yet determined what he was transporting or who he worked for."

Ben had no more to add, but he asked that Morgan keep him informed.

CHAPTER 15

DAN AUSTIN

A fter he left the coffee shop, Morgan decided to visit the local community college and talk to Dan Austin. It was only about six blocks away and a nice day, so he decided to walk.

Several men were gathered outside the funeral home. Morgan had played basketball with two of them in high school. He looked at the sign in front of the funeral home; it held the name of a coal miner who had recently been killed in a methane explosion. Morgan had once seen the results of this type explosion and knew there was not much to view. *Hell,* Morgan thought, *the results are worse than from a landmine.*

He also knew the miners were valued fighting men in infantry units. These men were accustomed to danger and hardship and would not run at the sound of gunfire. Working in the mines instilled a self-discipline that was valued in combat. Morgan respected their fighting abilities and at every opportunity would bring them into the fighting units he commanded.

He nodded to the group but spoke directly to Bert Combs and Pie Eye Johnson. "Bert, Pie Eye, how you doing?" Both miners had acquired that stoop-shouldered stance characteristic of working for a long time in a low-ceiling mine.

Bert and Pie Eye were a little bitter about their friend's death and blamed the lack of safety in the mine. They felt many of the required safety features had not been installed because they decreased mine productivity.

Morgan thought this was something the judge should hear about and made a mental note to tell her. He knew they'd told him because he'd do just that. Talking directly to her could get them fired. For them, he was a backdoor to the judge, and they knew she would look into it and, if necessary, have the safety issues corrected.

The conversation drifted as it always did to the big game they had played against Betsy Layne. The game always got bigger in the telling and now, for those who had played, it had gained legendary status. Just one more free throw, just one more stop, just one more basket. If only they had been able to stop the Tackett boy.

Morgan spent an enjoyable hour talking to his friends, but as he walked away, he remembered the game differently. The Tackett boy had scored forty-five points that night and killed them. But he had to admit it was a good game, for it was decided on the last shot of the game—by Tackett. It was a game everyone still remembered.

John David Tackett had gone on to play at Kentucky and was playing in the NBA. It was a game that Tackett also remembered, especially when talking to Morgan, who had guarded him that night. Morgan cursed under his breath, and then quickly looked around to see if anyone had heard him.

As Morgan walked down the sidewalk and was out of earshot, Pie Eye looked at Bert and asked, "You think he'll take the bait and challenge Tackett again?"

Bert watched Morgan. "Yep, he always does."

Morgan decided he needed to visit with Tackett again. He also would talk to the other deputies about the car that Tackett now drove, and he would have them call after they had stopped him.

As he continued down the sidewalk, he started to whistle.

Morgan knew Dan Austin but only as a nodding acquaintance. Austin had been a college professor at the local community college for about twenty years. He taught history and had an excellent teaching reputation but, according to the students, could be stubborn about giving an A. But the students seemed to appreciate his being demanding about their work. He had a reputation for being open and fair in his assignments and grading.

Morgan always thought that was high praise from students who were pretty good judges of character.

His father and uncle had held Austin in great respect. And Morgan always wondered why until, during one of their training sessions, his father told him about serving with Austin in Vietnam and how destructive he could be when aroused. His father rarely spoke of combat unless it was to make a point. Morgan still remembered the story.

They were running patrols out of An Khe into the jungle highlands near Pleiku when the battalion commander decided to set up a small firebase to lure the VC into attacking. Morgan's father was in charge of the reconnaissance platoon, since the lieutenant had been killed the previous week. He remembered the look on his father's face and the brutality of his words as he said, "About the only thing a lieutenant is good for is to show his men how to die."

The men he had lost had not been replaced, so he was too shorthanded to defend the firebase effectively. He placed his best men under Austin and put him in charge at the closest point to the jungle, figuring that was the most likely avenue of attack. He then coordinated with the artillery support officer on artillery fire registration and air support. Afterward he talked to the battalion operations officer to let him know his status and that they were going to radio silence and would only respond with radio clicks.

He knew if the attack came, it would be between 0200 and 0300 hours in the morning, so he lay down next to the sandbags, told the radio operator to wake him at 1100, and closed his eyes. At 1100 the operator shook him, and Morgan's father told him he would take radio watch and would wake him at 0200 for the expected attack. The radio operator merely nodded and also lay done next to the sandbags.

Morgan's father made the rounds of the bunker line to make sure half the men were asleep and half were awake. He informed Austin and the other squad leader that he wanted everyone awake between 0200 and 0300. He expected the attack at that time.

At 0200 he began to call for flares over his position. When the flares lit and began to descend by parachute, his father said he could see at least one hundred VC coming out of the jungle toward the firebase. As soon as the flares lit the night, rocket-propelled grenades from the jungle line began to streak toward the firebase.

He radioed that they were under attack by at least two companies of VC and asked for maximum artillery fire on the previous registration points, and he said he needed gunship support.

He had explained to Morgan that he did not want the VC to get close to his position. He wanted them at least a hundred yards away to prevent their bellying up to the firebase so they could not use artillery or air cover. His father said that the VC were experienced, resourceful fighters, and getting within thirty or forty yards of the Americans' position was one technique they had developed to counter the superior US firepower.

After the initial barrage of RPG rounds, he and the radio operator crawled to Austin's position. Austin had two killed and one wounded and was manning the machine gun himself and calling for more ammo.

The fight raged for another fifteen minutes as the VC slowly crept closer. Soon there were only ten left to defend the firebase. The VC made a final rush at the bunker line.

Morgan's father shook his head and simply said what happened next was amazing. Austin went crazy. He began to scream and race around the bunker line, recklessly exposing himself to enemy fire. He had a box of grenades and as fast as he could pull the pins, he threw them. The grenades exploded like mortar fire in the midst of the VC. They could no longer face the combined artillery rounds, gunship attacks, grenade barrage, and rifle fire and began to withdraw into the jungle.

Morgan's father said they later counted over forty VC in front of Austin's position. "I recommended him for the Distinguished Service Cross, but it was downgraded to the Silver Star. I thought he deserved more."

He had described the battle in a calm, matter-of-fact voice. Morgan did not completely comprehend the magnitude of a battle until after he had experienced it himself. Then he began to realize how utterly desperate, chaotic, and ferocious the battle must have been. He began to see Dan Austin with new eyes.

Several students were in chairs along the wall, waiting to see Professor Austin. Morgan knocked on the door, even though it was open.

He heard Professor Austin's gruff greeting, "Enter." He was obviously expecting a student.

Austin had changed much over the years. The sedentary life of an academic showed on his now sagging frame. He was bald with thick glasses. His white beard and sagging belly made him look like a wise uncle until you looked into his eyes. Those eyes gave him away. They were steel gray, bright, and as shiny as a newly minted bullet. This man could still be dangerous.

He came from behind his desk and warmly shook Morgan's hand. "Morgan, it's been a while. I had heard you were back. Looks like the Leandro woman has been taking care of you. They always do."

"Sir, it's good to see you also." His father had once told him to call Professor Austin sir, and through the years he had continued the practice out of respect for both Austin and his father.

Austin occupied a typical academic office. It was piled high with papers and books that spilled onto the cabinets packed closely along one wall. A computer was to his left. In front of his desk was a chair normally reserved for students, which he offered to Morgan.

Morgan carefully sat down, for the chair was infamous among the students. Austin had shortened the legs so that whoever sat in it had to look up at him. In addition, he had made the front legs shorter than the back to make the student feel even more uncomfortable. His father once said that Austin had copied this method of student torture from a navy admiral and thought it was quite effective.

They talked for several minutes about the school and the town before Morgan brought the conversation around to the body on Thornton Mountain. He asked if Austin knew anything about it.

Austin merely nodded and said, "I thought that might be why you dropped by and was wondering when you were going to bring it up." He explained that by organizing the student demonstration against drilling for gas, he was attempting to accomplish two things. First, he wanted to get the students interested in and aware of their civic responsibilities. Second, he was concerned about the future of clean drinking water, not only in the county but nationwide. He felt water was rapidly reaching the tipping point and that wars of the future may be fought over the control of clean water.

His main concern though was the toxic water left in the ground and not the backflow. He thought the judge was attempting to do a good job in making sure the backflow was properly handled and really had no concern in that area.

Morgan asked, "Is there anyone in your group that is capable of killing over this issue?"

"Morgan, look." He said, obviously exasperated, "These are students just spreading their wings. I just thank God that none of them know anything about killing. They will learn that soon enough."

Morgan responded that he needed to conduct a complete and thorough investigation and to follow the leads no matter where they led.

Austin said he understood, that he did not take the questions personally, and the he wished he could be of more help. He paused and looked at Morgan, and said, "There is one more thing. John Humphrey's girl has not been to class for several weeks now. This is highly unusual. She is a good student and shows a lot of promise in math and science."

Morgan knew that Austin took a special interest in students with promise and that he had an arrangement with the judge to make sure they received full scholarships to a university. Upon receiving the scholarship, they had to promise to come back to the mountains for at least five years. Morgan always thought that was a good deal for all concerned. It provided the students with an education while raising the educational level in the county, which had a ripple effect on the economy.

Austin added, "I've called Humphrey a couple of times but only got excuses and evasions. There is something wrong here, because Humphrey has always shown an interest in his daughter's education."

An itching sensation started on the back of Morgan's neck, for he had heard from several others that something was not right at the Humphrey farm. "Sir, I'll look into it. Other people have said something similar."

He stood up, shook Professor Austin's hand, thanked him, and left. As he walked down the hallway he knew he would have to come back for a more personal visit—perhaps to walk together downtown for a hamburger at the café, as his father used to do with Austin.

CHAPTER 16

MANNERS BOLEN

As Morgan walked back to the café to pick up his truck, he called Virgil and told him to meet him at the Mountain Grill for lunch.

Virgil inquired, "Who's buying?"

"Virgil, I always buy."

"OK, I'll be there."

Morgan laughed, for they had been playing the same game since childhood.

When Morgan arrived, Virgil was already seated, drinking coffee and talking with Jessica. She looked at Morgan and asked, "Is it true you are going to provide Virgil a Porsche for road patrol?"

Morgan looked at Jessica, then at Virgil. He turned to Jessica, "Well, we are considering an upgrade to our vehicles."

"You are both lying and going to hell." With that she swished off.

Virgil looked at Morgan, "Think we will get any lunch?"

They both laughed, and Morgan said, "Kind of difficult for the family to disown you." Jessica was another of their cousins.

The truth is, Morgan thought, *we are related somehow to half the county.*

Morgan eventually got his coffee and he and Virgil ordered lunch. Morgan took a sip and made a face. He muttered, "Damn family." The coffee was bitter and filled with salt.

Virgil laughed and said he thought that it may turn out to be a good day after all.

Over lunch, Morgan related his conversation with Professor Austin about the Humphrey girl not attending school and his attempt to gain information by calling Humphrey. Austin was concerned about Humphrey's evasions and felt something was not right. He then told Virgil about his conversations with the people in his intelligence network and their feeling that something did not feel right at the farm.

Virgil's only comment was, "Well, if it walks like a duck."

Jessica returned, put the sandwiches on the table, and left after favoring them both with a dazzling smile.

They looked at one another and quickly examined their sandwiches.

Morgan finally commented, "I think she's playing with our heads."

They continued to discuss the situation over lunch, raising various possibilities. Virgil finally asked, "OK, how do you want me to proceed?"

"We need more intelligence. Day after tomorrow, break out the ghillie suit and put the farm under twenty-four-hour surveillance. Talk to Ancil about relief. If you need anyone else, let me know, and I'll talk to Denver or Mason. However, no one is to know of their involvement."

He paused. "And Virgil, you work out the operational details to include communications. Come by the house tomorrow night for dinner and let me know how you are going to handle it."

Virgil nodded and left, leaving Morgan to pay the check.

Morgan decided to aggravate Jessica and left a large tip. On his way out, he smiled as if nothing had happened and told her he had never had a better cup of coffee. She smiled sweetly, for she knew he was lying.

It was about ten miles to where Manners Bolen now lived. While Morgan had been gone, Manners had bought twenty acres of hillside, bulldozed a large flat area, and built a large two-story house. People who had been inside said it was decorated expensively and in good taste.

When Morgan had left for Afghanistan, Manners had been a dopehead living on moonshine and barely making ends meet. He wondered where Manners had gotten all the money. *Almost certainly illegally*, he thought.

He parked the truck in front of Manners's house and blew the horn. Manners came to the door and waved Morgan into the house. As Morgan walked through the house, he looked around and, though he knew little about decorations, he thought they did look expensive.

They walked to the back porch that overlooked the hillside. Manners poured Morgan a half pint of moonshine, and they toasted each other.

Morgan took a sip and looked at the jar. "This is good moon, Manners—not like that rotgut you used to drink. That other stuff tasted like it had been filtered through a radiator. This tastes like it was filtered through charcoal."

Manners took a sip. "I've come up in the world, Morgan."

"I noticed that. A nice house, expensive furnishings, and good moonshine. Doesn't get any better than that."

"To the good life." Manners saluted with his glass and took another sip of moonshine.

"If you keep it up, Manners, even the good stuff will kill you."

"I know, Morgan, but once you start down the road, it's difficult to turn back."

Morgan looked at him and realized he was not talking about moonshine.

"It's never too late to turn back, Manners. We are kin, so if you need help, all you have to do is let me know."

"You are a good man, Morgan—too good for this sorry county. But it's too late, Morgan." He raised his glass again. "To the good old days when we were free to run the hills at night, hunting possum."

Morgan raised his glass in a salute.

"Why did you come here, Morgan?"

"There was a body found up on Thornton Mountain. Do you know anything about it?"

"I had heard it was Tim Mullen from the next county over. Why are you investigating it?"

"My jurisdiction, Manners. Did you kill him?"

"No, Morgan, I did not, but someone should have killed him a long time ago. I don't feel a bit sorry for him. I heard he liked to intimidate and beat women. I also heard he had raped a couple of women across the mountain, but I don't know who they were."

"Anything else you know about him?"

"I heard a rumor that he was heavy into meth and was running some sort of illegal transport business—most likely meth."

"Anyone specific I should talk to, Manners?"

"They were just rumors, Morgan."

They looked at each other.

Morgan said, "Whatever you are in, get out of it before it goes too far."

Manners simply shook his head and said again, "Too late, Morgan, too late."

Morgan looked at him again to make sure he was not too drunk to understand. "Don't make me have to come back, Manners. You know what will happen."

"With Virgil or Ancil?" Manners asked.

"Only if I have to. Don't let it come to that."

Morgan raised his jar, toasted Manners, took a sip, and set the pint jar down on the railing. He rose, shook Manners hand, and walked out.

As Morgan drove away, he shook his head, for he knew this was going to come to a bad end.

When he got to the bottom of the hill, he sat at the stop sign for a minute, thinking about his next move. Finally, he shrugged and turned toward the new house.

When Rachael arrived home that night, she found Morgan sitting on the porch overlooking the mountain, drinking chai and listening to Puccini's *Tosca* on the Bose player. When an opera was playing, she knew he was troubled. She went to the kitchen, poured a cup of chai, and joined him on the porch.

Without her asking, he began to tell her of his visit with Manners. He described the amount of moonshine Manners was consuming and his inferences during their conversation, which were disturbing.

Manners had indicated he did not know anything about the body on Thornton Mountain, and Morgan believed him. He also said that he had heard rumors that Mullen had raped a couple of women across the mountain but did not know who. He was unsure but felt Manners knew more than he was telling.

Morgan told her that Manners was into something illegal but did not want to talk about it. It was as if he were wishing someone would put an end to his activities. He ended by describing his feeling that this was not going to be a good ending.

Rachel looked at him with sympathy, for she knew how much he liked his kinfolk and how he always wanted to help them.

"Morgan, I love you and respect your feeling toward your family, and I do as much as I can to help them, but there are just some people in the world who will self-destruct, and there is nothing anyone can do about it—not even you, no matter how much you might want to."

Morgan realized how much she reminded him of his grandmother. They simply faced things as they were and not how they wanted them to be.

He pulled her into his lap. "I know you're right, but I still don't like it. You know I'll do what I have to, no matter if he is my kin."

Rachel hugged him, for she knew he would, no matter the cost.

CHAPTER 17

JOHN DAVID TACKETT

Morgan had just made the turn to go up the mountain when he received a call from Deputy Hopkins. "I've got Tackett stopped about a mile north of the Old Firehouse on the way to Pikeville."

Morgan said he would be there in five minutes. He quickly turned around, and his truck's dome light flashing, he sped north.

Unknown to Morgan, Deputy Hopkins had already alerted the dispatcher that he had stopped Tackett. The dispatcher had in turn alerted the town's informal grapevine that the game was on.

When he drove up, the deputy and Tackett were leaning against Tackett's car, which was a brand-new Audi R8. Morgan parked in front of the car, hopped out, and walked back toward where they were leaning against the car. They looked at each other, then grinned and shook hands.

Tackett commented with a smile, "I might have known it was you."

Morgan looked at the car and commented, "Nice car."

Tackett immediately responded, "A hundred and fourteen thousand dollars."

Morgan looked at his pants. "Nice pants."

"Two hundred fifty."

"They are paying you way too much for your skill level."

"Want to try me?"

"Follow me," Morgan said as he walked toward his truck.

The deputy turned toward his car and muttered into the microphone, "They are on the way."

Morgan turned on his siren and light and blasted down the road, followed by the Audi, followed by the cruiser with its lights flashing and siren sounding.

When they pulled into the high school gymnasium parking lot, it was almost full of trucks and cars, with others still arriving. Morgan parked along the sidewalk next to the entrance. Tackett parked behind him. Deputy Hopkins parked right behind him and then ran ahead and opened the door. The bleachers in the gym were almost full.

As they walked through the door, a roar filled the gym. It seemed the entire town was there. Morgan spotted Rachel and her mother at midcourt, two rows up in the bleachers. Morgan waved and both waved back.

Rachel's mother looked at her. "You think he's ready for this?"

"He has been back for months and has been working out almost daily. I think he's up to it."

The judge replied, "Well, ready or not it, was bound to happen. The town has been looking forward to this since Morgan returned, and so have I. How many times have they met?"

Rachel said, "Including the regional tournament, six times."

"Bet?"

"Ten bucks on Tackett." They both started laughing.

When they came out of the locker room, Tackett was dressed in his old Big Blue warm-up uniform, while Morgan wore the warm-up uniform of Logan County High School. The crowd roared its approval once more.

As they warmed up, Tackett shouted to Morgan, "I'm going to entertain them today." Morgan raised his arm in an Italian salute. The crowd began to whoop and holler.

Virgil came to meet them at the free-throw line in preparation for the one-on-one match. Virgil looked at them both. "One hour limit. Three sets of ten points each. Each man calls his own fouls. Big Blue has the ball." In all their previous meetings, Virgil could not remember a foul being called.

Tackett took the ball at the top of the circle, performed a jab step to the right, faked a shot, followed that with a ball fake to the left, and then drove right for an easy layup. Morgan had stumbled to the left, recovered, spun backward to the right, but it was too late. The crowd roared in its appreciation of a professional play.

This was the mountains; everyone liked their basketball. And Big Blue was the local religion.

Denver shouted from the sideline, "You've got him now, Morgan." Everybody started laughing, including Morgan and Tackett.

Morgan gave a knuckle to Tackett. "You are faster and trickier."

"I have to be," replied Tackett.

The first set went to Tackett. In the second set, Morgan began to bump, shove, and prod Tackett with stiff fingers. The play became exceptionally rough, with Morgan finally winning the set with a hip bump and a lay-in. Virgil called time for medical treatment.

Rachel quickly examined Tackett. "Just a cut lip and a bloody nose. You're OK to continue, John David."

He looked at her. "Rachel, if I had a broken leg, you would probably say the same thing."

She laughed. "Probably, John David."

Morgan had a cut above his right eye that was dripping blood down his face and onto his shirt. Rachel quickly stopped the bleeding, closed the cut with a butterfly clamp, and put a gauze patch over that. She grabbed him by the shirt with both hands, looked at him, and said, "Now get back out there and take it to him." She slapped him on the butt as he went back on the court. The crowd whooped with laughter.

At the end of the third set, the crowd gave them a standing ovation but remained in the stands as Rachel and her mother stepped onto the court. Her mother held up a ten-dollar bill between her thumb and finger. Rachel reached up, plucked it out of the air, put it in her purse, and followed her toward the door.

The crowd began to erupt with laughter and to call out recommendations to Morgan on how to handle his woman. Tackett put his arm around Morgan and laughed all the way to the locker room.

By the time Rachel arrived home, Morgan had taken a shower and was sitting on the porch overlooking the mountain, drinking chai tea, which he had acquired a taste for during his last tour in Afghanistan.

Rachel put her medical bag on the table and looked at the cut above Morgan's eye. "It will take ten stitches to close it properly."

"No shots."

Rachel began to sew up the cut.

Morgan finally muttered, "I can't believe you bet against me."

She stopped and laughed. "I won ten bucks from Mother. You were playing an NBA player, one of the best in the league. I know you have a big ego, but did you really expect to win?"

"No, but you could have bet on me."

"And lose ten bucks?"

"Damn, he is good. Faster, trickier, tougher, stronger. You know he gave me the second set and kept the third set close."

Rachel laughed and said, "Yes, but everyone had a good time. Take these pills and come inside. You are not going anywhere for the rest of the day."

Morgan grinned and followed her inside.

CHAPTER 18

THE HUMPHREY FARM

Morgan drove down the dirt road until he found the spot near the old dead tree and pulled into a tree blind so he could not be seen from the road. He sat in the truck, sipped a cup of coffee, and waited.

Soon Virgil stepped into the opening, pulled off his ghillie suit, and got into the truck next to Morgan. Morgan pointed to the thermos of coffee between the seats.

Virgil had been running surveillance on a meth lab for three days and smelled rancid. Morgan asked, "Virgil, is that your normal smell? I can see why you are having trouble with the lab technician."

"You know, Morgan. I just may have to take a bath sometime this month if I am going to make any progress. Unfortunately, there is this chief deputy sheriff that is either getting me involved in gunfights or has me sleeping in the woods."

"Virgil, things are hard all over. Now, how is the surveillance going?"

Virgil told him that Ancil still had eyes on the site to make sure nothing abnormal occurred while he and Morgan talked. He also said the meth lab was in the barn and seemed to be not only a manufacturing facility but also a transit point through the southeast states.

He passed along his list of vehicle numbers but thought that half of the license plates may have been stolen. Morgan studied the list and noted that most of the licenses were from Tennessee and Virginia, with several from North Carolina.

Morgan asked which way the traffic seemed to be flowing, and Virgil said he thought the traffic was flowing from Tennessee into Virginia. The trucks, mostly pickups with cabs, were loaded when coming from Tennessee but empty from Virginia, and cargo was transferred to the Virginia trucks.

Virgil said, "I'm not sure, but I think it's both weapons and meth for distribution up the East Coast."

Morgan replied, "Well, meth and weapons do make a lethal combination, so this may get real interesting."

Virgil simply nodded.

Morgan handed him a care package of food and more drinks and told him, "For you and Ancil. If you need more relief, I can talk to Denver or Mason."

"No, I can handle this with Ancil in relief. When are you going to take it down?"

"I think around noon on Wednesday. Have you noticed any other activity?"

Virgil said, "Yeah, there seems to be some activity about one hundred yards to the east of my position. Those occupying the position seem to be a little careless."

"OK, I want you on sniper over watch when we take down the farm. I'll send Ancil out Tuesday night to counter their activity."

Morgan got out of the truck with Virgil right behind him, reached into the back of the truck, and handed Virgil the .50-caliber Barrett rifle.

Virgil looked at him, nodded, and said, "Well, that should do it."

Morgan indicated that he wanted Virgil on overlook about six hundred yards up the hill from the barn, where he had a good view of the entire operation. He told him that if things broke bad, he was to take out the truck and car engine blocks and then stand by for any further target information. Morgan would control the target designation and indicate to Virgil the targets he wanted taken out.

They talked for several minutes about what Ancil would need to cover him in case of counter sniper activity. Then Virgil put on his ghillie suit, picked up the Barrett and packages, and disappeared into the woods.

"Morgan, Morgan," he heard someone say as he was nudged. He came instantly awake but realized he was not in Afghanistan, even though Ancil hovered over him.

He looked at the clock beside the bed. "Ancil, it's 0300 in the morning. What are you doing here?"

"Virgil sent me to report."

"How did you get here?"

"Why, like I always do. Across the mountains."

Rachel, sleepily said, "Morgan, who is that?"

"It's Ancil. Virgil has sent him to report."

"At 0300 in the morning? Ancil, you go back and tell Virgil…" Morgan put a finger over her lips.

"It's OK, Ancil. Let's hear your report."

"Virgil says the Humphrey farm is active with trucks coming and going a lot around 2400 at night. He has copied all the tags. People visit the farm mostly around 1400 in the afternoon, and he has taken pictures of them. He says to tell you that the only one he recognizes is Manners."

'OK, Ancil, anything else?"

"No."

"Go back and tell Virgil it was a good report for 0300 in the morning."

Ancil disappeared, making no noise.

Rachel rolled against Morgan, put her arm and leg across him, and muttered sleepily, "I'm going to kill Virgil the next time I see him."

The bed started to shake with Morgan's laughter. "It's something Virgil always did on our last tour in Afghanistan. It got so bad that whenever the colonel saw Ancil arrive at the HQ, he would stop the meeting and have Ancil report to me. After the report was over, he would simply resume the meeting as if nothing had occurred. The colonel was a good man."

"I've never known of a man to move as quiet as Ancil. He must have been of value to you on your last tour."

"Except for Virgil, he was probably my most valuable man." Rachel was the one person he did not mind talking to about the war. "Ancil is the best I have ever seen at silent infiltration and killing. I used him to make sure the Afghan warlords kept me informed of the movements of Al-Qaeda and the Taliban. We would kill Al-Qaeda wherever we found them, but I tried to handle the Taliban differently."

"I would go to their village and call for them to talk. I told them that if they did not cease their support of Al-Qaeda, he would kill one of their men that night, and I pointed to Ancil. They were brave fighting men, so they generally laughed and posted guards that night. Then I would have Ancil infiltrate the village and kill one of their men.

"The next day I would call for them to talk again. They'd laugh again, and I'd point to Ancil and tell him to kill two men that night. They'd post more guards. The next day I'd ask them to talk. They'd be grim but determined not to give in. I'd point to Ancil and tell him to kill four men that night. They'd post more guards.

"The next day I'd call for them to talk. There would be only frowns and worry on their face, but they still did not give in. I'd turn to Ancil and tell him to kill eight men that night. All their men would guard the village that night. The next morning you could hear the wailing of the women as the village came awake. The village elders would normally agree to terms after eight had been killed. They always wanted to know how I would protect them from Al-Qaeda. I pointed to Ancil and said he would kill them. They called him the Little Butcher."

Rachel tightened her arm around Morgan. "Brutal but effective." She fell back to sleep.

Morgan looked at her and shook his head in wonder.

CHAPTER 19

PREPARATION FOR A GUNFIGHT

On Wednesday morning, Morgan stood in front of the police conference room, which was filled with the ten deputies he had chosen for the raid. He knew he would have difficulty with those not chosen, but he knew he would include them on later raids. For this first major raid, he had chosen all combat veterans from Iraq and Afghanistan. Many of them he had recommended to Sheriff Harley. All of them had completed the one-month refresher course conducted by Virgil and Ancil. He was confident they all could carry out their assigned duties in the coming raid.

Morgan assigned five of the deputies to carry the new M-14 rifle chambered for the .30-06 and configured for both semi- and full-auto fire. That team would be under the control of Sgt. Campbell, who was a known and respected supervisor and marksman. They were assigned two half-moon areas around the building at a distance of 150 yards.

Between the two half-moon areas and the barn, he assigned the other five deputies at a distance of seventy-five yards. They would be armed with the M-4 rifle chambered for the .223 configured for fully automatic and three-round bursts. They would be under the command of Sallie Conley, who would also carry a LAW.

At the mention of the LAW, heads came up, and they looked at one another with that "oh shit" look. Morgan told them that each deputy would also wear an armored vest with ceramic inserts. In front of the group commanded by Sallie Conley would be Morgan with Sheriff Harley, who would carry both stun and fragmentation grenades. Again the deputies looked at one another.

Virgil would be on overlook with a .50-caliber Barrett while Ancil would act as counter-sniper cover. An emergency paramedic team would be positioned around the hill, out of the line of fire but available on command. Each man had a wired mike on a common communication channel but was expected to obey strict communications discipline.

The previous night, Morgan had discussed the operation with Rachel so she could take precautions at the hospital for casualties. This included bringing in two extra doctors along with additional staff. After discussing the operation with her, he decided to deactivate the cell towers covering that area to prevent outgoing calls and to cut the power to the farm.

After dinner, he picked up the phone and called the local telephone company manager, asking him to drop the cell towers in the area from 1200 to 1230 the next day. After several minutes of discussion, he still could not get the manager to budge without a court order.

Rachel, who had been listening to the conversation, put a finger over his mouth and took the telephone from him, identified herself, and began to speak to the manager about his family, wife, and children. After several minutes of conversation, she then asked him to implement the action that Morgan had requested. After several more minutes of discussion, she thanked him and hung up.

Morgan looked at her, and she said the manager would do it. She simply winked at him and went back to washing dishes while Morgan dried.

He smiled inwardly. The Leandro women had their fingerprints on almost everything.

Sgt. Campbell and the deputies with M-14s piled into two trucks while Sallie and the M-4 team loaded into a van. The emergency paramedic team followed in a white ambulance, while Morgan was in the lead truck with Sheriff Harley. Ancil had left about 2400 that night with night-vision goggles to provide security for Virgil.

Morgan performed a communication check with all deputies, then called Virgil to tell him they were on the way.

The raid team left the parking lot in convoy, and after hitting the main highway, went at speed toward the turnoff to the Humphrey farm. At 1150 they were driving on the blacktop road leading to the Humphrey farm.

Morgan glanced at the sheriff. "Any idea why John Humphrey is involved in this?"

"I don't know what to think. I've known Humphrey most of my life, and this is out of character for him."

At 1200 Morgan stopped the convoy around a curve and just out of sight of the barn. He made one last communication check with each team, alerted Virgil, and shouted into his microphone, "Go."

They drove at speed around the curve and toward the barn. At the 150-yard mark, the M-14 team peeled off and stopped their trucks in the designated half-moon area, scrambled out, and took position behind the trucks. At seventy-five yards, the M-4 team turned at a right angle to the road, stopped their van, and took position behind it.

Morgan and the sheriff stopped thirty-five yards in front of the barn and stood behind each door, which were armor-proofed to stop a 30-06 round.

Morgan shouted toward the barn, identified himself, and asked if Humphrey was in the barn.

A moment later, a strained voice asked if that was Morgan.

Morgan said it was and that he wanted Humphrey to come out and surrender.

Humphrey asked if Virgil or Ancil was out there, and Morgan said that they were up on the hill. Suddenly automatic rifle fire rang out from the hillside. At that, the sound of several people's laughter came from inside the barn.

Morgan asked Virgil how things were on the hill. Virgil answered that there had been a counter-sniper team active on the hill, with an emphasis on *had*. He indicated Ancil was glassing the area, looking for more targets, but they had accounted for the two-man team.

Morgan turned back to the barn and shouted that the counter-sniper team had been neutralized and asked again for Humphrey to surrender.

Humphrey asked if he could come out and discuss it. Morgan looked at the sheriff, who nodded. Morgan told him to come out.

Humphrey stopped about twenty yards from the barn door and was just beginning to speak when automatic fire came from the barn and ripped into Humphrey's back, knocking him forward onto the ground.

CHAPTER 20

GUNFIGHT AT THE METH LAB

Morgan yelled for covering fire. All the deputies opened up on the barn with fully automatic fire. Morgan ran in a weaving pattern to Humphrey, grabbed him by the back of his shirt collar, and dragged him toward the truck. Meanwhile, the sheriff and the deputies continued to pour automatic fire into the barn.

Morgan quickly examined the wound as Humphrey lay on the ground. When Humphrey looked at him, Morgan shook his head to tell him the wounds were fatal.

"John, how did you get involved in this?" the sheriff asked.

"I couldn't help it, Ben. They threatened my daughter if I didn't cooperate. I told them I would not get involved with them, so they kidnapped her."

"Is she still alive?"

"They let me talk to her at least once a week. But I don't know where she is."

Humphrey turned to the sheriff. "Ben, I need you to promise me something: get my daughter back."

The sheriff nodded, "Are there any other members of the family in the barn?"

Humphrey shook his head.

"Is there anyone from the county in there?"

Again Humphrey shook his head.

The sheriff started to ask another question, but Humphrey half sat up, vomited blood, lay back, and began to tremble. The blood and trembling finally stopped, and he lay still as his body settled into the slackness of death.

The sheriff looked at Morgan and said, "Kill them all."

Morgan nodded, activated his mic, and told Sallie to target the door with the LAW but not to fire until he gave the word. He then told her and the entire M-4 team that as soon as the LAW hit the door they were to rally on him. He then told the M-14 team to cover Sallie and her group as they ran toward the barn.

He turned to the sheriff and told him that after the M-4 team arrived, he wanted two fragmentation grenades through the door. The sheriff nodded.

He then told Virgil to knock out the vehicles and to kill anyone coming out the back. Virgil signaled an affirmative answer with two clicks.

Morgan and the sheriff crouched behind the truck as Morgan gave the command, "Sallie, lose the door."

Morgan heard the LAW go off, and the entire front of the barn disappeared in a tremendous blast that shook the truck and momentarily stunned both Morgan and the sheriff. Morgan looked for the deputies, who were running at full speed down the road toward the truck. He called for the M-14 team to provide covering fire, and they immediately opened up again on the barn.

When the deputies arrived, Morgan nodded to the sheriff, who ran forward and hurled two grenades, one after the other, into the barn.

As the grenades exploded, Morgan rose from behind the truck and started at a fast, crouching run with his rifle shouldered and pointed toward the barn. The five deputies, with Sallie on his right side, followed him toward the barn. Morgan entered the barn going straight ahead, while three deputies fanned to the left of the door and two fanned to the right of the door. All had their lasers on and were looking for targets. The rattle of gunfire filled the barn.

The men in the barn were tough and not as stunned as Morgan had hoped. They came up fighting. Morgan targeted one with his laser and put three rounds into him. He then switched to another and fired three more rounds. He caught a glimpse of men on both his left and right going down under the fire of the deputies. But the men in the barn were firing back, and he felt rather than saw two of his deputies go down.

Two men escaped out the back and fired backward as they ran across the field toward the tree line. One of them was suddenly flung like a rag doll as a .50 caliber practically cut him in two. Virgil was on the job, so Morgan turned back into the barn just as Virgil's rifle boomed once more. When he reentered the barn, the fight was over.

Morgan told Sallie and the remaining deputies to clear the barn and make sure everyone was down. He then called for the paramedics as he examined the deputies who had been hit. Both had received hits in the chest, but the bullets had been stopped by the ceramic plates. One deputy had also been hit in the arm, while another had been hit in the upper leg. The leg wound was spurting blood, so Morgan began to apply a tourniquet.

Sheriff Harley came through the door, and Morgan pointed toward the arm wound. Harley immediately began to attend to him.

The paramedics came running through the door, and Morgan indicated that his deputies were their first priority. The paramedics simply nodded and split between the wounded deputies.

Just then Morgan again heard the booming sound of Virgil's .50-caliber rifle. He keyed his mic and asked, "Virgil?"

Virgil said he had taken out the engines of two cars attempting to flee the scene.

Morgan immediately directed Sgt. Campbell, head of the M-14 team, to pursue and stop those attempting to escape. Several minutes later, he heard the sharp bark of pistols and the answering crack of the .30-06 rifles.

Sgt. Campbell reported that they had four men down—two dead, two wounded. He said one of the wounded might live. Morgan told Sgt. Campbell to keep him alive for interrogation.

Morgan tried to call the clinic on his cell phone but received no dial tone. He looked at his watch. It was only 1225. The fight had lasted ten minutes but had seemed longer.

Five more minutes until the cell towers are up. He reminded himself to visit the official who had agreed to take the cell towers down and thank him personally.

Morgan and Harley stood outside the barn, discussing the events.

"These boys fought awfully hard for a meth lab," Harley said. "I think this thing may be bigger than we thought."

"I think our first priority is to get the Humphrey girl back."

"I promised him, Morgan."

"I know."

Sallie reported that the barn was clear and that the deputies were stabilized and were going to be loaded for transport to the hospital. Morgan spoke to each of them as they were loaded into the ambulance.

He looked at his watch. It was 1230. Morgan called Rachel and told her what to expect and that he would talk about the operation tonight.

Sallie said she'd counted twelve dead gunmen: two were killed by Virgil with the .50 caliber outside the barn, seven killed inside the barn, and three were killed by Sgt. Campbell's team. She said that if treated, one of those wounded in the barn might live.

Harley looked at her and said, "Let him die." Sallie merely nodded and walked off, knowing the sheriff was in a foul mood.

By this time, Virgil and Ancil had come down from the overlook position. Virgil looked at the carnage then looked at Morgan and said, "You run a helluva operation!"

Morgan merely nodded and told him he was in charge of cleaning things up, searching the premises, and calling him about every hour to keep him informed. He added, "Sgt. Campbell may have one that is still alive. Have Ancil question him and let me know the results. He's awfully weak and will probably not survive the interrogation process."

From past experience, Virgil understood the implication.

Morgan and Harley got into the truck and drove away. It was time to brief the judge.

CHAPTER 21

GUNFIGHT AFTERMATH

They were in the judge's chambers and had just finished describing the raid, with a stenographer and the chief prosecutor taking notes. The judge had been querying them in detail of the raid in an attempt to make sure that their board of enquiry testimony would stand up. She finally turned to the chief prosecutor and asked if he had any additional questions.

"No, everything seems to be have been conducted according to the law. I'll convene a board of inquiry."

The judge thanked him and said that concluded the preliminary investigation. Then she asked both Morgan and Harley to stay behind.

After the prosecutor and the stenographer had left, the judge came from behind her desk and walked to a coffee decanter on a hutch. She poured a cup of coffee, put two sugars into the cup, and gave it to Harley. She then did the same for Morgan, but without the sugars. She poured herself a cup, took a seat in a small seating area, and asked both Harley and Morgan to join her.

She then looked at Harley. "Now tell me what really happened." He looked at Morgan and nodded.

Morgan then began a step-by-step narrative of what had transpired. He covered each step in depth to include the planning, the arms, and the ammunition. He mentioned the LAW and grenades, at which point the judge raised one eyebrow. Morgan answered they had gone heavy because of the suspected gun dealing; they did not want to be outgunned.

He then covered their discussion with Humphrey as he lay dying, Harley's decision to kill them all, and the attack on the barn. He talked about his killing of the two men in the barn, his deputies killing the other six inside the barn, Virgil killing the two outside the barn, and Ancil killing two more on the hill in back of the barn. He then covered the action of the M-14 group and the result of that action. He finally mentioned Harley's instruction to Sallie to let the wounded gunmen die and his instructions to Virgil on the interrogation.

She asked, "Have you heard anything from the interrogation yet?"

"Ancil has almost completed it. The Humphrey girl, along with several other girls, are being held at a safe house in Winchester, Virginia. There were to be shipped to the Middle East as sex slaves. Virgil says they should know more after Ancil finishes, but he didn't think the prisoner would survive the questioning."

The judge nodded and turned to the sheriff, "Ben, what are you going to do now?"

He looked at her and said, "I'm going to send Morgan to get the girl and bring her back if she's alive and kill everyone associated with kidnapping her."

She simply nodded, looked at Morgan, and asked, "What do you think you'll need?"

"I'll take Virgil and Ancil with me, but I'll probably need other support. I'll have a better idea after I do some research on the target."

At the mention of Ancil's name, she sat up straighter, if that was possible, and asked, "Virgil is bad enough, but do you really think that it's necessary to take Ancil? You know how he is!"

Morgan said, "Ancil is the best for what I need, and with the exception of you, Rachel, and Rosemary, I'm about the only other one who can control him."

She nodded and said, "Well, drastic measures call for drastic means. After you create an operational plan, come to me with your support requirements. In the meantime, I'll make a few calls and provide contacts in Virginia for anything your might need. Do not kill anyone associated with Washington before contacting me for a discussion."

She paused. "And one final question: do you think this has anything to do with the murder investigation?"

"Not directly, but I think there may be an indirect connection, and since Virgil saw Manners at the farm, the connection will most likely be through him."

She looked at both of them. "That is all for now. In the meantime, I'll try to put as good a face on this blood-bath as possible."

Harley and Morgan nodded and left her office. As they walked out of the building, Morgan turned to him and asked, "How far do her fingers extend?"

Harley, who had known her for over forty years, shrugged his shoulders. "Far, but how far I don't know. There are some things she has always kept close."

Morgan said he was going to the clinic to visit the deputies and to see Rachel. And so he did.

CHAPTER 22

WINCHESTER ASSIGNMENT

Ancil had learned from the interrogation that in addition to the Humphrey girl, there were fourteen other girls sedated in the building in Winchester, Virginia, awaiting transport to the Middle East, where they would be sex slaves. Each girl was being sold for $100,000. Because of its central location and access to east coast transportation systems, Winchester had become a way station for criminal activity.

The next day, Morgan did some Internet research and formed a tentative plan of how to attack the building where the girls were being held. His final plan would be based on on-site reconnaissance and an intelligence briefing.

He briefed the judge and Sheriff Harley that night on the results of the interrogation as well as his plan and requirements for retrieving Humphrey's daughter and the other girls. He figured he had at least two days of free activity before the personnel behind the slave trade would be alerted, because of the communication blackout imposed by the judge.

As the discussion proceeded, the judge became more and more agitated. At the end, she said, "Kill them all except those you need for interrogation. I will handle the fallout."

Harley and Morgan looked at each other and thought the same thing. *Damn, she is one angry mountain woman.*

For the next hour, she made the calls necessary to furnish Morgan the support he needed. He laughed silently as he heard the one-way discussion, for he had never truly realized the extent of the judge's influence. For the last several calls, she waved them out of the room.

That night she stopped by the house and briefed him on the additional contact points and telephone numbers. After she left, he discussed the coming operation with Rachel and, with her comments, refined the plan. He had always valued her insight into operational strategy and tactics. He thought, *She is a Leandro woman, after all.*

The next morning, Morgan picked up Virgil and then stopped to pick up Ancil. The three of them sat at the kitchen table at Ancil's place, drinking coffee, explaining to their Aunt Rosemary, Ancil's mother, what they were going to do.

As Rosemary heard about the Humphrey girl and the other hostages, she became scarlet with anger. She looked at each of them and with flashing eyes said, "Now, you boys do what is right and smite them with the sword of Gideon."

Morgan knew from experience that the women in his family were capable of extreme religious conviction that could easily lead to extreme anger and violence. Many were known to never forgive and to carry that anger to the grave.

He remembered sitting in the porch swing with his own mother one day when she began to tell him of a man who she felt had wronged her. She got red in the face as her anger steadily rose. Finally, he asked her if she would like him to visit with the man and read the good book to him. She looked at him strangely and said, "Why, Morgan, he's been dead for forty years." He had always felt the boys had inherited a streak of righteousness from their mothers and suspected that made them a little mean when anyone violated their perception of what was right.

Rosemary turned to Ancil and told him to bring the Humphrey girl back to stay with them. Ancil knew the girl, liked her, and nodded his agreement.

Morgan looked at Virgil and knew they were thinking the same thing: with only five years difference in age between Ancil and the girl, Rosemary was intending to do some matchmaking.

Rosemary packed Ancil a change of clothes, put them in a paper bag, and handed it to him. She then hugged all three and patted them on the shoulder. As they left, she again said angrily, "Now smite them mightily with the sword of Gideon."

Two hours later they stopped in Abingdon, Virginia, for gas and a sandwich. Ancil had asked him to drive by the cave were Daniel Boone had seen the wolves. It was the only thing Ancil had said since leaving the mountains, so Morgan drove slowly by the cave.

They were two hours up Route 81 before Ancil turned to Morgan and asked if he could interrogate the men who had taken the girl hostage. Morgan saw that Rosemary's anger had been passed to Ancil, and he would need to watch him closely. He said that he could interrogate only those he pointed out, but they were going to kill the rest. Ancil nodded in a satisfied manner, turned, and continued to look out the truck window.

As Morgan drove north, he reviewed the plan and the people he had already called. He looked at his remaining list and gave the Bluetooth a number to call.

At about 1500 that afternoon, they arrived at the Regional Government Training Facility just outside Winchester. The students training there had been moved to another facility in the middle of the state to undergo a two-day exercise. The director of the training facility took the three men on a tour of the facility but asked nothing about why they were there. His superior had called him the previous night and told him to expect Morgan, not ask any questions, and provide any services requested.

This had happened to the man one time before. He had done as instructed and had been promoted to his current position. He realized this was a black or partially black operation and that if it was successful and he kept his mouth shut, he would be promoted once again.

Morgan pointed out the rooms he wanted for the command and control center, the intelligence room, the operations room, the communication room, and the staging areas for the personnel who would start arriving that afternoon. He verbally gave the director a list of the groups and approximate times they would arrive that afternoon. The director immediately understood that nothing would be put in writing concerning this operation. Everything would be deniable.

CHAPTER 23

THE GATHERING

Morgan and his cousins, Virgil and Ancil, went to the command and control room, made some coffee, put the coffee in Styrofoam containers, and drove from the training center toward the hostage building to do an initial reconnaissance. It would simply be a drive-by with no stopping or extensive observation so as not to alert those guarding the girls. Morgan had asked a contact at one of the three letter-agencies for overhead satellite photos, on-site photos, a building plan, and a twenty-four-hour observation of the building to prevent any late surprises; he wanted to go in at 0300 the next morning.

As they drove by the building, Morgan asked Ancil about the two sentries on opposite ends of the rooftop. "Can you get to them?"

Ancil said, "Yes, but we will also need to take care of the overlook position."

Morgan looked at him questioningly, and Ancil said, "There is an overlook post on the forward slope of the mountain a thousand yards to the west. I think it's an early warning post for the building."

Morgan simply nodded and wondered how Ancil had spotted them. He knew that an early warning post also meant a control room in the building.

When they returned to the training center, the communications personnel had arrived and were busily installing the secure communications equipment to include the satellite downlinks. The intelligence officer for the operation had also arrived and was quickly putting the intelligence room into an operational condition. Morgan went to visit her while Ancil and Virgil cleaned their weapons.

Capt. Jennifer Raines, dressed in civilian clothes, greeted him warmly, for they had served together in both Iraq and Afghanistan. She was a slim, blond woman with intense blue eyes—and she was one of the best intelligence officers he had ever encountered. He briefed her on the operation and the intelligence requirements. She quickly grasped his intent and, as he talked, mentally formulated an intelligence plan.

He indicated that someone from the National Reconnaissance Office would be coming to handle the real-time satellite surveillance feed. She was always amazed at the organizations that Morgan had access to, but from their past operations, she had learned not to ask questions.

Morgan returned to the command and control room. Master Sergeant Earl Cummings from the Shooters was waiting for him. They greeted each other warmly, as old friends do. He looked at Virgil and Ancil, and said, "Might have known you boys would be here."

"Captain, I brought twelve Shooters and a four-man sniper team with me and all are armed as requested," Cummings said. "I selected them personally at the request of the colonel, who also told me not to ask too many stupid questions. The boys I brought are all senior grade sergeants with at least sixteen years' experience, and all have had four or more tours in Iraq or Afghanistan. You know most of them. By the way, the colonel sends his regards and wishes he were here."

"Is he as mean as ever?" asked Morgan.

"Hasn't slowed down a bit."

After several minutes of conversation about the colonel and the current status of his organization, Morgan and Cummings went to meet the Shooters selected for the operation. Virgil and Ancil tagged along behind them.

As soon as Morgan, Virgil, and Ancil walked into the room, it became silent. A faraway look came onto the eyes of the Shooters, for they recognized them and knew that the killing would soon begin. Morgan and his cousins were involved, so they knew it was most likely an unsanctioned black operation. Everyone looked at Virgil and the Little Butcher and knew they would need to keep their mouths shut.

Morgan met and spoke to each of them, greeting many by name and speaking to them of their common experience. On the way out, he nodded to Cummings in appreciation of his selection and told him about the meeting at 1800 that night.

Back at the C&C room, the National Reconnaissance Officer had shown up and was in discussion with Capt. Raines. The reconnaissance and satellite photos of the building and surrounding area, including the overlook position, had arrived and were being analyzed. In addition, hourly reports came in from personnel who were observing the building from various hides. They discussed her tentative findings, and she indicated she would have a full intelligence brief ready by the 1800 meeting.

Capt. Helu from the Virginia state trooper swat team was now in the C&C and in discussion with the Training Center director, who was shaking his head and saying he knew nothing.

Morgan had specifically requested Helu, who had served with the Triple Nickel in Afghanistan and had participated in several incursions into Pakistan with them. He greeted Helu and introduced Virgil and Ancil.

Helu looked at both of them, said he recalled them, and simply added, "Is this what I think it is?"

Morgan took him to one side and gave him a quick brief on the coming operation. Helu indicated he had brought the entire SWAT team and was armed as requested. Morgan asked for Cummings, who soon arrived.

Everyone knew one another from Afghanistan. They relaxed their guard and were blunt in their questions. Morgan told them to hold their questions until 1800, which would be a closed meeting with only selected personnel present.

Morgan also requested that the SWAT team and Shooters be kept separate and unaware of one another. They knew he wanted to compartmentalize the operation so that as little of the operation as possible could be leaked.

As they were talking, the commander of the local state trooper barracks arrived and introduced himself. He started to ask questions, but Helu shook his head, indicating they would talk later. The commander said that, as requested, he had at least ten units on standby. Morgan said he was to come back at 2100 that night for a detailed brief on his part of the operation. He also said that the operation was close hold and that there should be no communication outside the immediate group.

After the commander left, Morgan turned to Helu and asked how far the commander could be trusted with the details of the operation. Helu indicated he was a law enforcement officer with no experience in black operations. Morgan told him to expose only what he thought was necessary to satisfy his curiosity but not to expose any military or three-letter civilian associations with the operation. Helu readily agreed to that.

CHAPTER 24

THE ATTACK PLAN

At 1800 that night Morgan, Helu, Cummings, Virgil, Ancil, and Raines gathered in the intel room. Raines started her briefing by describing the hostages and what she knew about them. On the building blueprint, she indicated the location of the hostages and their probable condition. She then discussed the guards and indicated she believed them to be from the Horn of Africa, possibly Sudan, and they were all in the country illegally. She indicated their armament and possible location. She thought there were about twenty in the building but also that a transport unit may be arriving that night to move four of the hostages.

She then discussed their communications capability and its location. She indicated they were operating off commercial power, and she had not detected a UPS system. She then discussed the control element and its possible staffing. She covered the sentry and the overlook position on the mountain, and finally she indicated she could not detect any external alerts and did not believe the building was wired with explosives.

As she spoke, she constantly pointed to satellite images, photographs, and blueprints. After the briefing, she fielded numerous questions, primarily related to the armament and personnel locations. Everyone seemed to be satisfied with the briefing and answers. They knew the risks had been minimized as much as possible.

Cummings looked at Raines and said, "Captain, looks like you are as thorough as ever."

"Coming from you, Earl, that is a real compliment."

Virgil said, "Captain, can I kiss you now?"

Raines looked at him. "I see you are still as horny as ever."

Everyone chuckled. Morgan recognized they had started to bond as a team.

When the questions had stopped, Morgan began the operational briefing. At 0245 Virgil would take out the four people manning the observation post. He would have a thirty-minute window between communication checks to eliminate them. Morgan indicated to Virgil that he wanted them eliminated just after the communication check, with success indicated by four clicks. Virgil simply nodded.

A four-man sniper team, with silenced weapons, would then be established at the overlook position, under the control of Virgil. They would eliminate the targets designated by Raines, who would maintain a real-time satellite image of the building and its surrounding.

Morgan pointed to Ancil and indicated that at approximately 0255, upon receiving four clicks from Virgil, he would climb the southeast corner of the building and eliminate the two sentries on top of the building, make his way down the stairs to the bottom floor, and make sure the front door was unlocked. He was to eliminate any roving guards on his way down the stairway.

Virgil was to give two clicks when Ancil entered the building.

At 0310, when the front door was unlocked, Morgan would give the command to drop the power and communication to the building. In addition, the local cell towers would go silent for thirty minutes. No one bothered asking how this was going to be accomplished. All knew that someone with good connections was very pissed.

After the building went dark, the Shooters would leave the culvert and enter the unlocked door. Six Shooters would take the stairway to the second floor, followed by Ancil, the other six Shooters, followed by Morgan, would take the bottom floor. MSgt. Cunningham would accompany the Shooters on the first floor.

Simultaneously with entering the building, the barracks commander would establish a blocking position on all selected road exits. Morgan indicated the most likely positions but left the final locations to Helu and the barracks commander. The commander would maintain those blocking positions until personally relieved by Helu. Helu, along with Raines and Morgan, would brief the barracks commander at 2100. The barracks commander would have a contingent of ambulances ready to transport the girls along with doctors and nurses standing by to receive the hostages at the local hospital.

Morgan turned his briefing to the Shooters and indicated he wanted three men to lead, with two men following at a five-yard interval and the final Shooter ten yards behind, watching their six.

He looked at Cummings and indicated that he wanted everyone they encountered killed. On the initial sweep through the building, they were to bypass any locked rooms but to notify Helu of the locked rooms. The only exception was the control room and the sleeping areas. At the control room, they were to toss in a stun grenade then kill everyone except one. He was to be taken prisoner for later interrogation by Raines. Morgan did not want any papers moved or destroyed, since Raines and her team would sweep the building for intelligence while the prisoners were being freed.

In the guard sleeping areas, Morgan wanted fragmentation grenades and then everyone killed. Both shooting teams would then exit the building and, with an escort furnished by Helu, return to the training center, where an emergency medical team would be standing by for the wounded.

Upon the Shooters exiting the building, Helu and his SWAT team would then enter with one SWAT team element on the second floor and the second on the bottom floor. They were to clear and secure all rooms and the remaining people as necessary. He indicated the location of the dormitory hostage room and indicated that a segment of the Swat team was to stay and guard the hostages.

When the building was cleared and secured, Helu would give the all clear, and Raines and her team would sweep the building for intelligence. Simultaneously, Helu would call in the medical emergency teams to examine the hostages in preparation for the barracks commander escorting them to the hospital.

The one exception was a high-priority hostage that Morgan and Ancil would identify and handle.

The discussion of the operation lasted for another hour. No one asked about the high-priority hostage.

CHAPTER 25

ATTACK PLAN EXECUTION

At 0230, that night the operational elements were in place. The only change in plans was that the transport team had arrived early and was quartered in the building, most likely in the guard quarters. Morgan hoped they were lightly armed.

At 0245 Morgan and Ancil were in the shadows, lying on the ground next to the corner of the building. Each was dressed in a black Night Stalker outfit. Morgan was armed with a silenced MP-5/10 and a silenced HK-45. Ancil carried only his Fairbairn fighting knife. Each was dressed in a black watch cap with his face painted black.

At the four clicks from Virgil, Morgan tapped Ancil on the shoulder, and he started up the corner of the building. Morgan crawled in the shadows along the bottom of building, back to its front corner.

Virgil stood at the back of the sniper position and watched through a night scope as Ancil shinnied up the side of the building and slithered over the wall at the top of the building without silhouetting himself against the skylight. Virgil smiled and thought, *That little bastard is the best I've ever seen.* He didn't see the sentries disappear but did watch the door on the upper level open slightly as Ancil went through sideways. With two clicks, Virgil informed Morgan that Ancil was in.

Several minutes later, Ancil opened the front door. Morgan handed him a silenced MP-5/10 then gave the command to drop the power and cut communications.

He and Ancil stepped to one side of the front door just as the Shooters went through it. Six went to the right and up the stairs while Cummings and the other six went through the ground-floor door. Ancil followed the upstairs team while Morgan followed the first-floor team. He heard the clacking and popping sound of the silenced weapons as the killing began.

At 0320 Morgan was back at the front of the building as the SWAT team entered the front door. He and Ancil followed the team to the upper floor, since that was where the hostages were held. They were in a large dormitory filled with beds. Each girl was sedated through an IV. The Shooter medic was already examining the girls. She said they were fine and began to remove the IVs from each arm.

Ancil quickly looked at each girl until he stopped at one and motioned to Morgan. Morgan looked at the girl, who was about twenty, and knew the order to kill everyone had been correct. He indicated into his mic that the high-value hostage had been found, and a familiar voice replied that the ambulance was two minutes out.

Morgan held up two fingers to Ancil, who handed his weapon to Morgan, picked up the girl, and began carrying her through the building, with Morgan leading the way. Just as they exited the building, an ambulance accompanied by a state police car entered the parking lot and stopped in front of the building.

The back doors of the ambulance opened, and two women dressed in EMT uniforms stepped out and pulled a mobile bed from the ambulance. Ancil placed the girl on the bed while the other two covered her with a blanket, strapped her down, and loaded her into the ambulance.

It was then that Morgan noticed the two EMTs were Rachel and her head nurse. She and the nurse entered the ambulance. Ancil also stepped into the ambulance and looked at Morgan and said, "Ma said for me to bring her home."

Rachel heard this, looked at Morgan, and nodded. Just before he closed the door, Rachel looked at him and winked. He suddenly felt good and started laughing to himself.

He went around to the left side of the ambulance to talk to the driver. It was Denver. Morgan asked how he happened to be involved in the operation. Denver replied that had been trying to figure that out ever since he became conscious while driving north on Route 81. The only thing he remembered distinctly was Rachel asking for a favor. Mason was in the passenger seat and started laughing.

Morgan asked if they were armed. Mason lifted two MP-5/10s and said they were courtesy of Sheriff Harley. At a tap from the inside of the ambulance, Denver immediately put the transmission in gear and waved to Morgan as he drove off, being led by a state police car.

Helu, the commander, and Raines came up with their report. Two on the SWAT team were wounded slightly but in no danger. Fourteen hostages were being looked after by doctors until the arrival of the ambulances, which would transport them to the hospital. There were twenty-two dead bodies inside.

Morgan indicated that Helu was now in charge of the scene. He took Helu to one side and told him to keep any mention of the Shooters and three-letter organizations out of it. There was also to be no mention of himself, Virgil, Ancil, or Raines; it was strictly a state operation. Morgan told him that when he was finished, he was to come to the training camp. With that, Morgan and Virgil got into the truck and drove off.

As he drove back to the training center, Morgan called the judge and Harley and updated them on the operation. He indicated the number wounded, the number rescued, and the number killed. He then indicated the Humphrey girl was on her way home with Rachel and that he would provide a detailed brief once he got back.

CHAPTER 26

SPARKLE GAYHEART

Morgan had been back from the Winchester assignment for three days and had briefed the judge and the sheriff on the operation. There was a meeting scheduled for the next day in the judge's office to continue their discussion of the operation and to deal with the sex slave trade. He knew that the fallout from this operation would continue, for the judge was still angry at the attempted sex slave operation in her county and fully intended to hunt down and eliminate the other cells. Morgan knew he, Virgil, and Ancil were going to be her instruments.

He had made recommendations on commendations for Cummings, Helu, Raines, and the camp director. He knew the judge would make the necessary arrangements to recognize each individual appropriately. Since it had been a black operation, he also knew the commendations for Cummings and his team would be made in private. The judge, he thought, would see that Raines was put on a fast track for promotion to major. Helu would be suitably recognized, and the camp commander would again be promoted.

Morgan had lunch with Virgil at the Mountain Grill that morning and mentioned that he intended to continue his investigation into the murder on Thornton Mountain by crossing the mountain to see if Sheriff Bailey in the next county could provide additional information on the murdered man.

Virgil was unusually quiet during the breakfast. Morgan looked at him, laughed silently, and wondered if there was trouble in the love nest.

After lunch, Morgan drove across the mountain. When he arrived, Sheriff Bailey was there to greet him. Bailey said, "Heard you and the Tackett boy put on a good show a couple of weeks ago."

Morgan muttered something unintelligible and sat down. Bailey grinned and sat down behind his desk.

Bailey's secretary brought two cups of coffee, and they began discussing the killing on Thornton Mountain. Bailey indicated that Tim Mullen had not had a permanent job but nevertheless seemed to have a steady income. He took a lot of trips out of state, and Bailey thought someone was paying him for it. Bailey did not know what was being transported, but it was most likely illegal. Mullen was known to be a hard case and to like a fight but had no criminal record. He seemed to like intimidating and beating up women. Bailey had heard rumors that he occasionally raped them, but no one had ever brought charges.

"Too scared, most likely," Bailey concluded.

"Anyone of particular interest?"

Bailey looked at him intently. "I heard some rumors, so you might want to visit the Gayhearts. I know they are some distant kin to you, but Birdie and her girls are not real talkative."

Morgan thanked him and decided to make the Gayhearts his next stop. The last time he had been there was with his grandmother more than three years before. His grandmother had heard that the Gayhearts were having some difficulty and wanted to visit them. She, like Rachel, tended to look after their kinfolk.

He called his grandmother and briefly talked to her. He knew that she, in turn, would call the Gayhearts.

Morgan turned onto a dirt road that led up to the Gayheart house. The yard was well tended and the front porch clean and decorated with flowers. He remembered the Gayheart girls as being lively, intelligent, and attractive. They never wore the best clothes when they were young, but that hadn't seemed to bother them or, as he recalled, the boys that were constantly hanging around. In fact, he could never recall seeing an ugly Gayheart woman. The oldest girl had even gone on to become a model in New York.

He walked up the steps and knocked on the door. It was opened by Sparkle, the youngest of the Gayheart girls and perhaps the most attractive, if that were possible.

They looked at each other until she broke the spell by coming forward and kissing him on the cheek.

"Welcome home, Morgan," she said softly in a mountain lilt. "Your grandmother called, and we've been expecting you. Come on in. Mom is in the kitchen and has your coffee ready." All the women in the family knew how Morgan liked his coffee.

He greeted his cousin Birdie with a hug and drew back and looked at her. "Now, which daughter are you?" he asked. Both Birdie and her daughter laughed with pleasure.

"Morgan, you take after your daddy, God bless him. He had the tongue of a Welsh poet, especially around women." Morgan's father had often recited poetry to the family, especially when woman folks were visiting. His mother had been as enraptured as the other women.

Morgan knew that Birdie was complimenting him and appreciated it, but he knew he was different. The woman did seem to like him, but the men kept their distance. His grandmother, not given to sentimentality, once said, "Morgan, you are a loner. Now live with it. You will never have many friends, but you will be able to count on the ones you do have."

Morgan smiled at the thought. His friends could be counted on two hands, and they were mostly family.

Sparkle and Birdie looked at each other and thought, *Morgan is entertaining himself again.*

He sat at the kitchen table, sipped his coffee, and enjoyed the company of Birdie and Sparkle. Both women liked to talk and were intelligent and well-read. He always liked being with them, and they knew it.

Finally he looked at them and said, "Tell me about Tim Mullen." Their faces instantly changed.

Birdie said, "Morgan, I think you want to speak to Sparkle alone." She rose and quietly left the kitchen.

Sparkle refilled Morgan's cup and sat across from him. She sat back in the chair, crossed her legs, and looked at him. She had always liked him and was comfortable discussing private issues with him.

She had been to the roadhouse halfway up the mountain, enjoying the country and western music and drinking beer with her friends. Tim Mullen had come over and asked her for a dance, which she had refused. He had become angry and loud, and he had called her a Gayheart bitch who thought she was too good for him. She had a temper that she could not hold in check and had retorted that he was a thief, a coward, and liked little boys and girls. At that his face had gone white, and he'd left the bar.

She had left the club around midnight, gone to her car, and began to unlock the door when someone grabbed her from behind and held a knife at her throat. It was Mullen.

Morgan sat stoically, sipping his coffee. He nodded for her to continue.

Mullen had taken her to a van, torn off her clothes, raped her, and threatened to kill her, her sisters, and her mother if she told.

He asked, "Did you report it?"

"No, I came home, took a shower and a morning-after pill, and talked about it with my mother."

"You know he was found dead up on Thornton Mountain."

"Yes, I had heard," she replied. She stared at Morgan and fairly hissed with anger, "I'm glad the son-of-bitch is dead."

He was not surprised about this. The mountain women held their emotions in check, but they could be utterly unforgiving.

She put her hand on Morgan's arm, "Did you kill him?"

He looked at her. "No, but if I had known about this, I would have." She nodded and knew he meant it, for they had been close several summers before.

He asked, "Did you discuss this with anyone else?"

"No."

"Let me talk to Birdie."

As she got up to get her mother, Morgan got up as well, took her by the shoulders, and pulled her into his arms. She came willingly and wrapped her arms around his neck as he lifted her off the floor. He whispered in her ear, "You should have called me."

She drew back, looked at him, buried her face in his neck, and replied, "You had just returned and had not yet recovered."

Morgan hugged her tightly and then slowly lowered her to the floor.

When Birdie came into the kitchen, Morgan was sitting there, gazing out the window. Birdie took a seat at the table and waited for him to return.

When Morgan finally looked at her, Birdie said, "Morgan, you are the only man I know who can break a woman's heart and still have her love him."

"She will find someone who loves her in the way she deserves."

"I hope so, Morgan. I hope so."

"Birdie, tell me who you talked to about the rape."

She crossed her arms, looked directly at him, and told the story.

Later that night, when Rachel and Morgan were in bed she rolled next to him, put her arms around him, kissed him, and said, "I hear you went to see the Gayhearts today."

He told her about Tim Mullen raping Sparkle Gayheart and the story that Birdie Gayheart had told him.

She slowly kissed him again. "I'm not surprised. What are you going to do?"

"Nothing. I'm going to sleep."

She pulled herself partially on top of him, kissed him harder, and whispered, "Later."

CHAPTER 27

FAMILY RECKONING

As Morgan and Virgil had driven back to Eastern Kentucky, they had discussed the results of Capt. Raines's interrogation and its implications. Both were surprised and disappointed with one of the findings.

They had been fortunate to keep alive the leader of the cell. He had been wounded by one of the grenades, and Morgan knew that the best time for interrogation was while an individual is still feeling the aftershock of the violence.

During the chemically enhanced interrogation, the cell leader had broken and divulged the entire cell operation for six of the eastern states: Kentucky, Tennessee, North Carolina, South Carolina, West Virginia, and Virginia. Unfortunately, he died before he could elaborate on what he knew about the other states. Morgan felt unsatisfied with the interrogation, since he wanted to know more about that cell's relationship to the surrounding cells. He knew that would be difficult, because cell organizations depend on isolation, with little or no contact between them.

The next morning at 0800, he walked into the judge's office, where she and Harley were having coffee. Morgan walked over to the coffee service, poured a cup, sat down, and without prelude began to discuss the events of the last three days.

After he had finished, the judge looked at him and asked if he was sure about Manners. He nodded. She then turned to Harley and asked what he thought. He said that Morgan's finding sounded about right, but that Manners ought to be questioned about the activities in other states, the overseas transportation, and any possible overseas contact points.

She looked at both of them and said that the activities were extending beyond what she had originally thought. Then, in that hissing sound she made when really angry, she said, "People have no business coming to my county and killing and kidnapping my people—the very people I have sworn to protect." When she or Rachel used that sound, the hairs on the back of Morgan's neck always stood up.

She turned to Morgan and asked him what he wanted to do about Manners. He had known Manners since they were children, hunted with him, and lived across the hill from him.

Morgan looked at her and Harley. "I intend to call Orville." At that, both the judge and the sheriff looked at him.

"That is drastic," said Harley, who had also known Manners since he was a child. "You think we need an action that extreme?"

Morgan replied, "I think he also knew about the rape of Sparkle Gayheart and did nothing about it. That and his activity in the sex slave trade have taken him outside the protection of the family. He is a blacksnake."

The judge knew Manners as well and had heard the tale of Morgan's grandmother and the blacksnake.

She nodded, "Manners has made his bed with our family. Now let him lie in it. However, you will need to talk to your grandmother about this."

"I'll visit her afterward," replied Morgan.

At the conclusion of the meeting, the judge indicated she wanted to think about any follow-on operations dealing with the cells in the other states and overseas.

Harley and Morgan left her office and walked across the street to the County Café for lunch. Virgil was waiting for them when they arrived. They took a booth in the back of the café.

Molly always seemed to keep that booth empty when they met in the judge's office, for she knew some sort of decision had been made and its ramification played out in the booth. She poured their coffee and walked away. They were her kinfolk, and that was enough.

As they sat drinking their coffee, waiting for their sandwiches, Morgan began to discuss the decision with Virgil and the plan for implementing that decision. For the next hour, the discussion and planning continued over lunch.

After Harley had left, Morgan looked at Virgil and asked him what he thought. Virgil shrugged, looked up from his sandwich, and said that Manners had brought it on himself. He then began to recount the story about their grandmother and the blacksnake. Morgan liked this story and, like the judge, had heard it many times, so he simply sat back, drinking his coffee, and listening to Virgil's mountain drawl.

Their grandmother, along with her brothers and sisters, had been out hoeing hillside corn when she ran across a nest of rattlesnakes in a tree stump. In their midst was a blacksnake. She proceeded to kill the rattlesnakes with her hoe and afterward looked at the blacksnake, shook her head, and killed it also.

After the day's hoeing, they were sitting at the supper table, discussing the day's events, when she told them what she had done. One of her brothers looked at her and wanted to know why she had killed the blacksnake, since they, along with the cats, helped control the vermin in the corncrib. The grandmother looked at her brother and replied in a Scottish brogue, "I cotched it in bad company."

After finishing the tale, Virgil went back to eating his sandwich. Morgan smiled and took a sip of coffee.

That night after supper, he and Rachel sat at the table for several hours, discussing the events of the last few days and the options for the follow-on operations.

He reviewed the discussion in the judge's office, and they extensively discussed only one action, which dealt with Manners Bolen, who had been implicated as one of the cell leaders. Before going to bed, they had agreed that the option decided upon was justified.

He followed her to bed after he had called Orville.

Morgan and Virgil knocked on Manners's door. When Manners opened it, he looked at Morgan and Virgil, nodded at them, and said, "I been expecting you boys ever since I heard about the events up in Winchester. I assume the judge sent you?"

At that question, Morgan simply nodded.

Manners invited them in and got a quart of moonshine from the refrigerator and three pint-sized jelly jars. They sat on the back porch, drinking moonshine and discussing the good times they'd had running the hills at night, hunting possum.

When the conversation paused, Morgan looked at him and asked, "Why did you do it, Manners? These are your people."

Manners looked at him and, in a hesitant tone, replied, "Money, Morgan. I got greedy."

Virgil merely nodded.

Orville was waiting for them when they arrived. He stood with his thumbs through the straps of his bib overalls, chewing a cud of Brown Mule tobacco. He had on a dirty bill cap with an unintelligible inscription. His face was covered by a beard, and he had on long, red underwear under his overalls.

Orville looked at Morgan, then at Virgil, then at the tarpaulin in the truck bed and asked, "Is that the feed for the hogs?"

Morgan nodded and wondered why he insisted on calling these deliveries "feed."

Orville continued. "I ain't fed the hogs in the last pen for a couple of days, so they'll eat anything." He paused. "Well, I did feed them some coal, but that don't count."

Morgan backed the truck to the last hog pen and lowered the tail gate. Orville climbed into the truck. He removed Manners' shoes, belt, buttons, and anything he did not want the hogs to eat, and placed them in a burn bag. Once he had removed everything, he said, "Now, you boys know he was kin?"

Virgil said simply, "He was a blacksnake."

Orville nodded. "Grandma sure is somethin', ain't she?"

Morgan and Virgil nodded, for that was one thing the entire family always agreed on.

Virgil took the arms and Orville took the feet, and they threw the body into the hog pen. As they turned their backs and walked away, the hogs began to grunt and squeal.

Morgan and Virgil got into the truck and sat there for a moment. Then Morgan started the truck, paused, then looked at Virgil. They nodded to each other, and Morgan drove back down the road.

Both knew they were going to be fully employed for the next year.

FINIS

27244990R00102

Made in the USA
Charleston, SC
04 March 2014